A FABULOUSLY UNFABULOUS SUMMER FOR HENRY MILCH

MARSHALL THORNTON

Published by Kenmore Books

Edited by Joan Martinelli

Cover design by Marshall Thornton

Images by 123rf stock

ISBN: 978-1-0880-2300-6

First Edition

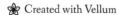 Created with Vellum

ACKNOWLEDGMENTS

I'd like to thank Ben Starkey, Amy Barrett, Jeanie Williams, Tina Greene-Bevington, Nathan Bay, Randy and Valerie Trumbull, Jenna McGrath, Brian Fagan, Chris Carter, Jennie Evenson, Shanee Edwards, Danielle Wolff, Robyn Paris, and, of course, my editor Joan Martinelli.

CHAPTER ONE

My Nana Cole claimed she couldn't remember a blessed thing about the night she had the stroke. I found that incredibly annoying since it meant, eventually, I'd have to come out to her all over again. Okay, I want to be fair. I didn't *just* tell her I was gay. I sort of blamed her for all the violence in the world done against queer people and called her stupid. It might have been a little much.

So you can see why I might not want to go through that again. I mean, it was traumatic even before I called 911. If I told her I was gay a second time she might spontaneously combust. Or worse, go all Carrie on me and attack me with telekinetic flying knives.

No, thank you.

Of course, she could be lying. She probably *was* lying. Lying runs in our family like a bad overbite. Or, she might *not* be lying. Certainly if she did remember that night, it was hard to believe she wouldn't blame the entire near-death experience on me.

Her stroke *wasn't* my fault. But it was easy to imagine her deciding my being gay was such a horrible bit of news it had given her the stroke. I mean, there was my whole people-like-you are the scourge of the earth—

Well, enough about that. She recovered. Or mostly recovered. She was in Midland Hospital for nearly three weeks before being transferred to Brookhaven Fields Rehabilitation Center, where she was asked to do all sorts of demanding things—like putting together the kind of fifty-piece puzzle you'd ask a five-year-old to complete or, and this was equally challenging, putting round and square pegs into the appropriate holes.

The first week or so, she had trouble speaking. She slurred and drooled and chewed on her words as though they were Chiclets. I really had no idea what she was saying most of the time. But then her speech became clearer, and a month later it was very nearly what it had been. She did still occasionally pause—as though she were trying hard not to stutter—and then skip forward quickly. Kind of like when a CD skips.

She was released from the rehab on the first Wednesday in June. The sun was out in full force that day, and there were few clouds in the sky. The temperature hovered just below seventy. It was the kind of day we had often in Los Angeles, though rarely in Northern Lower Michigan, and it made me feel homesick. To be honest, most things made me feel homesick.

Nana Cole had to sign a few forms and then an orderly, who was in his mid-thirties and Black—something which made him stand out like an over-bright neon sign in Wyandot County—pushed her in a wheelchair out to her Escalade which I'd left parked in front of the entrance. Gently, he helped her climb into the passenger's seat and told us to have a blessed day as he closed her door.

Walking around the SUV—only limping a little on the ankle I'd badly sprained six weeks before—I climbed into the driver's seat.

When I was all the way in, Nana Cole said, "He was... nice." There was a heavy dose of surprise in her voice.

"You mean even though he's Black?"

"I didn't say that." She waited a moment then added, "But, yes. Even though he's Black. When you see them on TV they're so angry."

"You shouldn't believe everything you see on TV."

"I meant... the news. The news is real."

Having seen the news she watched, I didn't entirely agree. I decided to leave that alone, though. I thought we should get all the way home before we had yet another argument.

As I pulled away, I turned on the local NPR station, which mainly played classical music. It was the only station I could stand since the top forty stations were basically an episode of *American Idol* and there were zero stations playing club music. A piece ended and the news came on. The big story of the day was that Martha Stewart had been indicted on nine counts of insider trading or some such.

Nana Cole grumbled and I thought for a moment she might have another stroke. She loved Martha Stewart. She had a subscription to *Martha Stewart Living* and faithfully watched her TV show. As the story ended, I resisted the temptation to say, 'And that's a good thing.'

The next story was about scientists genetically altering chickens to give them teeth.

"That's horrible," Nana Cole said.

"The chickens?" I asked, since she could have just been late reacting—

"Chickens are awful creatures. Teeth... would make them worse."

"How would you know?"

"I used to raise chickens. When your mother was a girl." She was silent a moment before she added, "The eggs were nice."

Having had enough of the news, I reached over and pressed the tuning button until I found a country station.

"Oh, that's George Strait," she said, with a half-smile. It could have been George Bush for all I knew. I tried not to pay attention. I'd only put it on to be nice.

I suppose the drive from Bellflower to Masons Bay is scenic. I mean, if you like trees and water and sky. I wasn't entirely sure how I felt about all that. Everything had looked extremely dead when I'd arrived in February—which had matched my mood—and it continued to look dead right up until about Mother's Day when the trees began aggressively sprouting leaves.

We had trees in Los Angeles, where I'd spent most of my life, but they never seemed to lose their leaves. They never looked dead. Or I didn't remember them ever looking dead. One or the other.

I should probably explain myself. I went to a party at the beginning of February. A great party. Full of A-list gays. Or at least B-list. You know, industry types. I wanted to have a good time, so before I went I took a Vicodin I'd gotten from a girl at work when she wasn't looking.

Later, at the party, someone offered me an Oxy. I think it was a 10, but I could be wrong. It might have been a 20, or even a 40. And I might have gotten one from someone else later, though it could have been something else entirely. That part's very fuzzy.

The thing is, I don't remember leaving the party or when I got home. Sometime in the early morning, my roommate, Vinnie, found me on the living room floor barely breathing. Or so he claims. Seriously, I love Vinnie to death, but he's not the most truthful person in the world.

Anyway, 911 was called, and when my mother showed up at the hospital I was 5150'd (which, if you ask me, is a form of legal kidnapping). Three days later I had to decide between my grandmother or rehab. I chose my grandmother.

Possibly the wrong choice.

"Oh my God, what was that?" I nearly screamed, as we passed by some roadkill smushed in the center of the road. "Was that somebody's cat?"

"Don't be... stupid. It was a possum."

"Ah, well, that's better," I said. I was getting used to constantly seeing deer and various other forest creatures dead by the side of the road. They were apparently not very bright when it came to crossing the street. But the idea of someone's cat—

"Possums aren't as gross as you think. They eat ticks. Bev told me."

"Bev would know," I said. She was my sometime boss at the Wyandot Conservancy. She tended to know a lot about the local flora and fauna. I guess I was supposed to feel bad about the dead possum, but I couldn't muster the emotion.

"Cats are bad for the, uh, world. Nature."

"Because they don't eat ticks?"

"I don't remember. I just remember Bev telling me... they're bad. Barn cats. Not inside cats."

Anyway, my grandmother's farm was on West Shore Road right outside Masons Bay, a small—and I do mean small—town right below Michigan's pinky, on the knuckle.

I say farm, but it really wasn't anymore. Not like it was. There were still two cherry orchards on either side of the long driveway, which she leased to her neighbor Jasper Kaine, who had a large orchard of his own, and with whom she split the profits. The rest of the property, though, was given over to nothing more than a few vegetable gardens that would remain fallow that year. She'd dropped hints about my doing the spring planting, but I chose not to hear them.

"Oh look, my lilacs," Nana Cole said, meaning the three large pinkish blooming bushes by the house. Then she seemed to fold a bit. "I missed the tulips."

There had been daffodils and then tulips while she was in

the hospital and rehab. I suppose I could have been a better grandson and brought her some. Unfortunately, it hadn't occurred to me. I suppose it should have.

"How do the cherries look this year?" she asked me.

"I dunno."

"You didn't go out to the orchard to look?"

"No. And I wouldn't know what to look for if I did."

"For one thing, whether there are a lot of them."

Honestly, I didn't know what would constitute a lot, so I didn't say anything as we drove down the driveway to the two-story, white clapboard house with its large, stone porch—made of what I'd learned was called river rock. Many of the older homes in Masons Bay used these rocks, which had been tumbled in nearby rivers until they were smooth and round.

Reaching Nana Cole's house, there were four vehicles sitting there in the driveway. As I parked her Escalade, I noted that the cars belonged to Bev, Jan, Dorothy and Barbara. All friends of my nana's. As soon as we parked, Reilly, her six-year-old yellow lab mix, came running.

"Why are they standing outside?" Nana Cole asked. "Why haven't they gone inside?"

Except they couldn't have because I'd taken to locking the doors. I said so and got a very dark look for my trouble.

"Why on earth... would you lock the door?"

"Because I nearly got killed just a few feet away."

"That's not going to happen twice," she said, somewhat exasperated.

Rolling my eyes, I said, "I'll grab your walker out of the back."

I jumped out of the SUV and ran around to the rear. Reilly traced my every step, jumping up on me twice.

"Down boy," I said, secretly pleased that he liked me so much. He had really become my dog in the last few months. I was trying to figure out how I could bring him back to L.A.

with me when I left. Which I hoped would be as soon as my grandmother was able to live alone.

I popped open the back and reached in for Nana's metal walker. Before I could get to her, she'd opened her door and was climbing down. She snatched the walker out of my hands and then, thrusting it in front of her in a dangerously uncontrolled way, headed toward the house.

I tried telling her to slow down but was drowned out by her friends greeting her. Each of them held a casserole dish, some kind of small-town custom I just didn't get. Casseroles in hand, they'd come to see me after Nana first had her stroke.

It was a custom that made me feel as though I had no idea how to feed myself. Actually, that wasn't far from the truth. I'd been distressed to discover there was no such thing as delivery in Masons Bay, and that the nearest McDonald's was a thirty-five-minute drive. I felt like Robinson Crusoe.

Staring at Nana's friends, I remembered I'd never returned the baking dishes they'd brought the first time round, which made me wonder how many baking dishes did these women own? My grandmother and I couldn't be the only people in Wyandot County in need of casseroles.

"Emma, slow down, we're not going anywhere," Bev said.

"I'm sorry, my bone-headed... I'm sorry Henry locked the door."

I wanted to say again that I was nearly killed just a few feet away, but they all knew that.

Barbara said, "You know what it's like in the city. Those habits are hard to shake."

Nana Cole came to an uneasy stop so she could turn and look at me. "Well, unlock... the door. Let them in."

I gently eased Reilly down, and as I did, said, "No one ever tried to shoot me in Los Angeles."

"That you know of," was my grandmother's retort. "They probably just missed."

While I was glowering at her, we clambered inside; me

and five women over sixty. This was now my life. Horrible thought.

Immediately, the women began rearranging everything. They installed Nana Cole at the table, fusing over her to make sure she was comfortable. The kettle was put on the stove. One of the dishes wasn't actually a casserole—better yet, it was a coffee cake. The casseroles went into the fridge, while the coffee cake landed on the table after being cut into bite sized squares.

My dishes from the night before weren't washed—okay, I admit it was several days' worth—which earned me a snide look from my grandmother. Without asking, Jan began washing them.

"Henry will do that—" Nana Cole said.

"Mooch, Nana," I corrected her. Preferring my nickname.

"Oh, don't be ridiculous," she said to me. We'd been through this before. Then to her friend, "Jan, stop."

"It's no trouble," Jan said. "It'll take me half a second."

"I didn't know we were entertaining," I mumbled.

"You don't have to be embarrassed," Barbara said. "Men are hopeless at housework."

I resented that and would have said so if it weren't so obviously true in my case.

Questions were asked about Nana Cole's health, some subtle, some not. While the women chatted, Bev took me aside and asked, "Do you think you'll be coming back soon? I have a stack of inspections that need doing."

"Oh, um, yeah. I guess. I mean, as soon as it's safe to leave my grandmother alone."

And I had no idea when that would be. It wasn't that I didn't like the job with the conservancy, it was... well, no, I guess I didn't like it. It was a lot of tromping around wetlands and working farms and the kind of places I'd never deliberately go to. You literally had to pay me to wander around in the woods. And even then...

"Oh my God, what are you talking about?" Nana Cole said suddenly. The room went dead quiet. Everyone turned and looked at me. The kettle on the stove began to whistle.

"What?"

"You didn't tell her?" Bev asked.

"Tell her what?"

"About Reverend Hessel."

"What about Reverend Hessel?"

"He was killed. During a robbery," Dorothy jumped in.

"Oh."

Well, how was I supposed to know? I really hadn't seen anyone for weeks except my grandmother and her caregivers. I didn't read the *Eagle*, Mason Bay's weekly newspaper. Nor did I watch the local *9&10 News*. Basically, if it wasn't on my Yahoo! start page or on NPR I had no idea it had happened.

I can't say I had any fondness for Reverend Hessel. I'd only met him twice. Once at a pancake dinner and then at the hospital a few days after Nana Cole had her stroke. I'll never forget the way my grandmother's eyes lit up when he entered her hospital room. She said a few garbled words, so I explained, "They're optimistic about her regaining her speech. Maybe even fully."

"Oh, that's wonderful," he said as he sat down on the side of her bed. Smiling, he said to her, "Emma. Dear Emma. You have nothing to worry about. God would never give you more than you can handle. You're going to come through this with flying colors."

He took her hand in his and asked, "Would you like to pray?"

She said, "ehsssh." Which was actually a big improvement over the day before when she'd been saying "eggggg" instead of yes.

Reverend Hessel turned to me, but before he could ask me to join them in prayer, I said, "I'll wait in the hall."

Standing in the hallway, I started thinking about God not

giving us more than we can handle. I didn't believe it for a minute. I mean, what about the people who'd jumped out of hundred-story windows on 9/11? Did God think they'd just handle it? Or the people Jeffrey Dahmer killed? Or Jews being ushered into gas chambers? Seriously, I could spend all day coming up with examples of God giving out far more than people could handle.

Reverend Hessel stayed in the room with my grandmother for about ten minutes. Once I stopped making a mental list of horrific tragedies God could have chosen not to give us, I spent the rest of the time staring at the walls in the hallway. They were mint green on top and a dirty pink on the bottom. Every ten feet there was a painting of sandy dunes at a beach.

Not for the first time, I asked myself *why?* Why would anyone think pink and mint green were soothing colors? I mean, did they really think you'd stand there thinking, 'my loved one is dying, but the walls remind me of sherbet, so it's okay?'

When Reverend Hessel came out he caught me off guard, and before I knew what he was doing, he had my hand in his and seemed not to want to let it go.

"If there's anything I can do for you, please let me know."

"Thank you."

"I know church isn't something you're into, but we're always there for you. God is always there for you."

Instead of looking at him, I was looking at his shirt. I noticed that he wasn't as pudgy as he used to be. I was tempted to ask if he'd been going to Weight Watchers, though he'd probably just tell me he'd prayed the pounds away. I realized he was waiting for me to say something.

"My grandmother seemed happy to see you."

"She's one of my favorites. So feisty. I'm glad the doctors are optimistic."

"Me too," I said, finally pulling my hand away.

Jan turned the burner off under the teapot. She got cups

out of the cupboard. I glanced at Nana Cole, who looked a not-very-optimistic ashen gray.

"When did it happen?" I asked, about Reverend Hessel's murder.

"Last Thursday," Bev said. To my grandmother she added, "I didn't want to tell you. I was concerned about your condition. I still am."

"When is the funeral?" Nana Cole asked, her voice hollow.

"It was on Monday."

"I missed it? Was it nice?"

"It was lovely."

"Good. I thought Reverend Hessel was such a kind man," she said. "It's a shame. A terrible shame."

"I don't understand it," Jan said. "I mean, I understand why Reverend Hessel would try to stop them, but why would someone steal from a church in the first place?"

"Well, for the money," I said, stating the obvious. But then, quickly, it wasn't all that obvious. "Wait a minute. You said, Thursday. Why would you steal from a church on a Thursday?" They each stared at me, clueless. I suspect they had trouble getting past 'Why would someone steal from a church?'

I continued, "Think about it. The big money day is Sunday. The collection money probably goes into the bank on Monday. Was there some kind of event that Wednesday? A reason someone might think there'd be money lying around?"

Apparently not, since no one said anything.

"Do we know anything else?" Nana Cole asked.

"The news reports have been very thin," Bev said.

"People are talking about it," Barbara said. "They're just not saying much."

"I heard he was beaten to a pulp," Dorothy said.

"Emma doesn't need to hear the gory details," Bev admonished her.

"What kind of person beats a minister to death?"

"If he was severely beaten it implies anger," I said. I'm sure the information came from *CSI* or maybe *Diagnosis Murder* one or the other. "That doesn't sound like a robbery."

"Well, there wouldn't seem to be any other explanation," Barbara said.

"Did they break in?" I asked. "That's one way to be sure it was a robbery."

"The doors of the church are *always* open," my grand-mother said, pointedly.

"It's terrifying to think whoever did this is still out there," Dorothy said. "Our minister. None of us are safe."

"Henry will go and have a talk with the sheriff," Nana Cole volunteered.

"No I won't."

Ignoring me, she told her friends, "He has a good relation-ship with Sheriff Crocker after solving the Sammy Hart murder."

Nothing could be further from the truth. Just the week before I'd picked up my reward, which had included a photo op, one that would likely show up in the *Eagle* soon. It hadn't gone well. And...

Ugh! The reward money. Now there's a disappointment— more about that in a minute. But before I left, the day I picked it up, Sheriff Crocker sidled up to me and said, "I hope you're planning to take that money and leave town."

Well, that had been exactly my plan, but he sounded like he was telling me to leave town. I wasn't so great at being told what to do and then there's the fact that—

Nana Cole was giving me the evil eye, so I said again, "No. I said, no."

"We'll talk about it later."

CHAPTER TWO

As soon as Sheriff Crocker handed me the reward check I glanced at it and was completely horrified. They'd taken taxes out. Who does that? That meant instead of fifteen thousand dollars, I received eight thousand, nine hundred and forty-two. Apparently, they decided to tax me as though I made fifteen thousand a week, which I most certainly did not.

Sure, I would get a lot of it back if and when I filed a tax return—except I wouldn't be filing a return. My student loan was seriously in default, and I had it on good authority that the IRS would not send you a refund if that was the case. Sucks, right?

Not to mention, I hadn't actually seen any of the money yet. It hadn't made sense at all to open a bank account in Michigan since I did not intend to stay more than another few weeks. Months? Oh God, I was trying not to think about that.

Anyway, using a deposit slip from the back of my checkbook, I'd made out the deposit and mailed it off to Bank of America in California. It should get there any day now.

Of course, it's still enough money to get a decent second-hand car but not much else. And that's only if no one else gets to the money first.

And yes, it was a very real possibility the money might get taken from me. Two days after I was given the check, I'd gotten a phone call from Los Angeles General Hospital—yes, the same General Hospital shown every afternoon for those of you who enjoy soap operas. Someone named Robbie Hale. My first question was, "How did you get this number?"

"Your mother gave it to us," Robbie said. "She's your emergency contact."

"This is not an emergency."

Ignoring me, Robbie—who I think was a man, though it might have been a woman who smoked heavily—said, "You're responsible for your bill: Twenty-seven thousand, five hundred and eighty-three dollars. How do you intend to pay it?"

"I don't. Call my mother back and ask her for the money."

"She said you would be responsible."

"See, here's the thing. I was 5150'd, put into your hospital against my will. Essentially, kidnapped and held hostage. You should be paying me. Damages."

"You have no insurance?"

"I worked as a barista. Nine dollars an hour plus tips. No insurance, no vacation, no sick days—"

"And what do you do now, Mr. Milch?"

"Mostly, I'm taking care of my grandmother who recently had a stroke."

"Can she pay your bill?"

"Let me put her on."

I held my flip phone to my chest for a moment and then did my spot-on imitation of my grandmother in the days following her stroke, "Hewwo, naaway aper mingle whip cwwwee..."

"Very amusing. I'm sure your grandmother appreciates the imitation. Could you ask her to pay your bill?"

"No. I'm not going to do that."

I mean, seriously. Would I accept twenty-five thousand

dollars from her—yes, in a heartbeat. Would I turn it over to a freaking hospital? No, absolutely not.

I decided it was an opportune moment to hang up on Robbie, which, for a brief moment, reminded me that it's so much less satisfying to hang up a flip phone than it was a desk phone or even a wall phone. You just don't get the same bang for your buck.

After Nana's friends left, I straightened up the kitchen just to prove a point. I peeked at each of the casseroles and asked my grandmother which one she'd like for dinner. She chose the tuna casserole. I turned on the oven and slipped it in. As I did, I began thinking about money again.

I suppose I didn't have to spend *all* the money on a car. I could imagine getting around Wyandot County in a car that cost a few thousand. I could even imagine getting around L.A. in a car that cost that. What I couldn't imagine was driving from Masons Bay to Los Angeles—through gigantic mountain ranges and sizzling deserts—in a cheap used car. Something could easily go wrong. Something was *likely* to go wrong, and cost me every cent I had left. Or land me in the middle of some B-grade horror movie scenario: Extremely attractive city boy's car breaks down in the front yard of a family of cannibals.

It could happen.

Oh, and then I remembered car insurance. And registration fees. (Necessary if you didn't want to get arrested by some aviator-wearing sheriff in a backwoods Texas town.) I had no idea how much those things cost in Michigan. Or Los Angeles, for that matter. My mother had taken care of all that.

The best part of her breaking up with whichever boyfriend she happened to be seeing was that she often didn't want the things he'd given her. My 1990 Honda CRX had been a gift to her from Frank, who she'd been with from 1991 to 1996. They broke up just in time for her to give me the car as a high school graduation gift. Except, of course, she didn't really give it to me. She just let me use it all through college right up until the time she 5150'd me. I wondered what she'd done with it? If I flew to L.A., would she give it back?

"I'm serious about Sheriff Crocker," Nana Cole said as I fed Riley a can of dog food, which he practically inhaled. He really was a disgusting eater.

"So am I," I said. "I'm serious, too. I'm not going to talk to him."

"I'll give you five hundred dollars," she said, and I had the uncomfortable feeling she'd been reading my mind. Five hundred wouldn't make a lot of difference, but it would—

"Why?" I asked. "They said it was a robbery gone wrong. Why isn't that enough?"

"You don't believe that. You don't... think it was a robbery. You said so."

"Two thousand."

"What!?"

"You offered five hundred. I'm negotiating."

"One thousand."

"Fifteen—"

"No. One thousand. Take it... or leave it."

Well, I thought, *at least she won't take taxes out.*

THE NEXT NIGHT, the Tony Awards began at eight after a repeat of *60 Minutes*. I was entranced. Nana Cole was less than pleased. They kept mentioning *Hairspray*, which she couldn't believe didn't take place in a beauty parlor—not that she thought a beauty parlor was a good location for a musical. About a half-an-hour in they did a number from the show. When Harvey Fierstein joined in my Nana Cole frowned at me and said, "That's a man in a dress. Singing."

"Oh. Is it?"

"I'm done. Help me to bed."

Which meant I missed the end of the number and the next twenty minutes of the awards. After I helped her get ready for bed—by pulling a nightgown over her head and then accepting her clothing as she stripped each piece off underneath, thus preserving her modesty—she said, "So... you haven't... seen the sheriff yet."

"It's Sunday."

"It's the sheriff, he works every day."

"I'll go tomorrow," I promised. "I'm going to take Reilly out and then I'll lock up."

"Lock up? Why would you—"

"Someone murdered your minister. I'm going to lock the doors."

"I don't know what this world is coming to," she muttered.

"Oh yeah," I said. "I forgot, 'And then everyone locked their doors' is the first line of Revelations."

"Oh, it is not. Don't talk... foolish...ness."

I managed to avoid seeing the sheriff for three more days. Getting involved seemed like a bad idea. Seriously, I *did* nearly get killed. But then, a trip to the sheriff's office in itself wasn't dangerous. To my ego, maybe, but other than that it was basically safe. Finally, I decided to go—mainly so my grandmother would stop harassing me.

The sheriff's office was located in the Wyandot County Municipal Center on the first floor. Along with the sheriff, the recently constructed building—yellow brick with squinty little windows—housed the county clerk, a court, senior services, county treasurer, the board of commissioners, and a raft of other departments. I knew all that because I read the board on the way in.

I decided not to bother Sheriff Crocker at all. Instead, I went directly to Detective Rudy Lehmann, who'd once been a detective in Grand Rapids. For some reason that impressed people.

The Wyandot Sheriff's Department featured one whole

detective to investigate everything from vandalism to murder. Since that still didn't amount to a lot of crime, I was able to find Detective Lehmann sitting in his cramped, messy office.

In his early forties, the detective had brown eyes that were sad rather than kind, and a receding hairline. He wore a wrinkled gray suit that was probably out of style before it was made.

While I had no reason to think that he liked me any better than Sheriff Crocker, he hadn't suggested I leave town, so it seemed logical I might get more information out of him.

"Hello. My grandmother wanted me to come by and ask a few questions about Reverend Hessel's death."

The sheriff would have said something about my grandmother being good people, and then given me a look that suggested I wasn't. But as I said, Lehmann was from Grand Rapids, so there were a lot of social niceties he didn't bother with.

"Oh, well, if your grandmother sent you I guess I'll have to tell you everything."

I ignored his comment and launched right in, "It doesn't make sense to me why the Reverend was killed during a robbery on a Thursday. There wouldn't have been any money in the church."

Lehmann raised an eyebrow at me. "And a meth head would have thought that through?"

"Meth head? You think it was an addict trying to get money for drugs?"

I could tell he was uncomfortable having given me that much information. I stood there in the doorway to his office attempting to square what I knew with what he'd just said.

Of course, I was familiar with meth or crystal or Tina as the boys called it. Personally, I didn't much like it no matter what it was called. In L.A. tweakers were everywhere. As far as I could see, Tina was a disaster. She gave you acne, rotting teeth, a nasty chemical smell, and to top it all off made you super horny.

Can you imagine? You had to go out and try to get laid with bad teeth, bad skin and a bad smell. Definitely not for me. Yes, I like the occasional sedative. But my skin is flawless.

"Is there a big meth problem around here?"

"Big enough."

"How much money did they get, do you think?"

"I can't give out that information," he replied.

"So, none," I guessed.

He narrowed his eyes at me, inadvertently telling me I was right.

"If they didn't get any money, why are you so sure it was a —" I stopped. There was a reason he thought it was a robbery. And that a meth head had done it. Something must have been left at the scene. Paraphernalia? A glassine envelope? A pipe of some kind? But why? Why would you try to burgle a church and when you didn't get any money leave some of your gear behind. That didn't make sense.

"It was someone physically strong, wasn't it?"

"Why do you say that?"

"Because Reverend Hessel was beaten to a pulp."

"He wasn't... He was struck in the head with a blunt object. Three times."

Now we were getting somewhere. Unfortunately, he added, "That was in the newspaper."

"Oh," I said, a blush jumping into my cheeks. "I guess I missed that. What kind of blunt object?"

"A blunt one."

"Something that the killer brought? Or was it something that was there in the office?"

"We don't know what it is, so we can't figure that out."

I chewed on my lip as I concentrated. If this were *CSI* the shape of the wound would tell us it was ballpeen hammer, possibly a particular brand. So, if the wound wasn't telling them anything, it was just, well... flat?

"What about physical evidence? Fingerprints? DNA?"

"Of course we found fingerprints. Lots of fingerprints. Problem is, the list of people who'd been in and out of that office is about two pages long. We could spend a couple of weeks eliminating prints to see what we're left with, but the remaining prints wouldn't be useful if that person isn't in the state police database. Generally, you need to be a criminal in order to be in there."

"What about DNA?" I asked.

"DNA requires bodily fluids, fingernail scrapings, hair... and, once again, if the DNA isn't in the FBI database it's not going to do us any good. Until we have a suspect."

That was not helpful.

"So, do you have a suspect?"

"Look, just because you got lucky with the Sammy Hart murder doesn't mean you know anything about investigating crimes. Tell your grandmother we're working on this and expect to have more information in a couple of days."

"And you'll call her to let her know?"

"It will be in the newspaper."

———

TECHNICALLY, I was not supposed to leave Nana Cole alone—something her doctor had insisted I *must not* do—really, did he think I'm completely irresponsible? I'd been able to go to the sheriff's office because her physical therapist was scheduled to come by at one. Nana Cole had hustled me out of there at ten-of. After I visited the sheriff's office, I went to Benson's Country Store and picked up a few things. Well, more than a few things. My grandmother had given me a long list.

So, at nearly three, I walked through the back door juggling four plastic bags. Nana Cole sat at the table with an old guy around forty. He was certainly not my idea of a physical therapist, but whatever. Each to his own.

I shoved the bags of groceries onto the counter, and said, "Hi, I'm Mrs. Cole's grandson. I thought you'd be finished by now."

"Henry, this is Jasper Kaine," Nana Cole said. I remembered the name. He was my grandmother's neighbor who leased her cherry orchards.

"Oh, sorry, I thought you were the physical therapist."

"No, she's long gone," Nana Cole said. "You're going to need to call tomorrow and have them send someone else."

I couldn't deal with that—seriously, she could use the telephone herself. I was trying to get a good look at Jasper Kaine. I'd only ever seen him from a distance. He was husky and dark with flinty eyes. I'd noticed that he didn't bring a casserole when Nana had her stroke. I mentioned it to her once and she'd said, "Well, he's a man. Men don't do those things."

I have to admit, I'd been relieved that I'd never have to make a casserole for anyone's trauma.

Jasper stood up and shook my hand, saying, "Nice to meet you, Henry."

Then he sat down again. He looked like he had a lot of muscles underneath his Polo shirt. I tried to focus on a spot above his eyebrows. Truth be told, he was exactly the sort of guy I used to let buy me drinks at Revolver. Sometimes I'd let them do more than that.

"You can call me Mooch," I suggested. It had been my nickname since high school.

"Why would I do that?"

"Jasper is catching me up on the cherries," Nana Cole said. "He says the Rainiers have come in strong this year."

He nodded, saying, "It should be a good crop."

I had no clue what a Rainier was. Obviously, it was some sort of cherry, but that was as far as I got.

"After you pick them, you'll sell them on the side of the road?" I guessed. There were fruit stands here and there around the county. They were already selling rhubarb and asparagus. Though, how anyone made a living doing that, I had no clue.

He shook his head. "Our main client is a company outside of Detroit. They pit the cherries, bleach them, dye them and soak them in sugar to turn them into maraschinos. After that they're either bottled or covered in chocolate and boxed."

Hmmmm. I have to be honest. Growing up my experience of cherries was a bit scant. I would have them in Shirley Temples when my mother took me to singles bars in the afternoon—only when she was between boyfriends. I don't remember it being a regular thing. I mean, I don't remember *everything*—

And of course, my mother didn't cook. We either went out to eat or had take-out. There were cherries in the cans of fruit cocktail she sometimes bought me. I loved cherry cough drops and was always happy when I got sick enough to ask for them.

The thing is, I don't remember ever having a real live actual cherry like the ones my grandmother grew. I had no idea what they really tasted like.

I wanted to go upstairs to my room. I needed an Oxy to get me through the long boring afternoon. I have to say, it had been lovely while my grandmother was in the rehabilitation center. I'd go see her for a couple hours in the morning and then I was free to do whatever in the afternoon. Whatever was usually one or two 10s. Well, not *usually*. Every other day, maybe. I mean, I didn't keep a chart or anything. I just didn't do it *every* day. Addicts do drugs every day. I just like to have fun. Cue Cyndi Lauper.

My grandmother had introduced me to Dr. Blinski, who was an absolute treasure. All I had to do was show up every two weeks, pay him sixty dollars for an office visit, complain that my ankle was just not getting any better, and he'd write me a new prescription for thirty ten-milligram Oxycontin. Then I'd be off on my merry way.

"You also have two acres of Sweetheart cherries," Jasper said directly to me.

That got my attention. "They're not *my* acres. They belong to my nana."

He looked a little confused, like he knew something I didn't. But—come on, there was no way my mother would keep the farm. She'd probably just give it to some guy she was dating. It was never coming to *me*.

Besides, what would I do with it?

"Well, things are looking good," he continued. "We got through the frosts reasonably well. We've got a shot at a good harvest."

"Let's hope," Nana said.

They both seemed nervous, but I didn't get what the suspense was about. You plant trees, they sprout fruit, you pick it. Didn't sound like rocket science to me.

Jasper stood up, making a scrapping noise with the chair. He reached out his hand to shake mine—again. I shook his hand, feeling the heft of it, the dry callouses. It was a man's hand through and through.

"It was nice to meet you, Henry."

"Yeah, you said that already."

"Henry," Nana Cole chided.

"Well, he did."

This all made him chuckle in a way I didn't quite get. Fortunately, he was out the door a moment later, leaving me alone with my grandmother.

"So, I went and talked to Detective Lehmann," I said, leaving it dangling there in the air.

"And?"

"He didn't want to tell me much, but this is what I found

out. He thinks Reverend Hessel was killed by a meth addict with a blunt instrument during a burglary attempt."

"That makes sense, doesn't it?" She seemed very pleased.

"I'm pretty sure there wasn't any money taken, though. Detective Lehmann wouldn't say, but I think if there were money taken, he would have."

"Why does that matter?"

"I don't think a meth addict would forget the money. They'd be desperate. I mean, even if all they got was whatever was in the reverend's pockets. They'd still have taken it."

"A drug addict is probably not very smart."

There was a bit of sting in that. If I were a drug addict I might have been offended.

"He didn't want to tell me whether the blunt instrument was something already in Reverend Hessel's office or something the killer brought with him."

"What difference would that make?"

"Well, if the killer brought the blunt instrument with them, then they planned to kill Reverend Hessel. Which does imply it was someone who knew him. If they used something in his office, then it was likely spontaneous. Which might still be someone who knew him or—"

"Yes, but you said it was a burglar. They didn't expect Reverend Hessel to be there. So it had to have been... spontaneous."

I wanted to say, 'In that case what did they use and where is it?' Instead, I said, "That's probably right."

Pleased with herself, Nana Cole smiled and said, "It's tourist season. It was probably someone from out of town."

"So, you're thinking it's someone who came up planning to hike and buy fudge and go boating, but at the last minute decided to add 'kill a reverend' to their itinerary?"

She gave me a withering look. Seriously, I felt my roots die.

"Is that all you found out?"

"He didn't really want to tell me anything."

"Well, that's not worth a thousand dollars."

"You're going to welch on the deal, aren't you?"

"It's just not a lot of information."

"I asked him to call you when he found out more."

"And is he going to?"

"Absolutely."

CHAPTER THREE

I don't belong here. This is not where I should be.

I had those thoughts a lot. Seriously, I was completely wasted in Masons Bay. I suppose you'd call me a twink. Now, in case you don't know, a twink is a young guy, thin, with excellent hair and mucho sex appeal. Some people use the term derisively, comparing us to the famous, over-processed snack cake. But since there are a whole lot of attractive men interested in twinks it's not so bad.

Unlike a classic twink, my hair was brown (though sometimes I went blond), my eyes were brown and soulful (I get told that a lot) and my features symmetrical. Well, they were symmetrical until I'd smashed my face into a steering wheel. My nose had not yet recovered.

Tragically—since I was nearly twenty-five—I would only be a twink for a few more months. I really had no idea what I would do. The only plan I'd been able to come up with was moisturizing more and lying about my age.

I had no plan B.

Anyway, the next morning it was cold and raining, so I made Nana Cole oatmeal. It seemed like a good idea and it was simple, you just follow the directions on the package. I added butter, milk and some raisins I'd found in the pantry. I should have known, though. When I set it in front of her, she looked at it as though I'd done it all wrong. Honestly, it didn't look *that* bad.

"Is there any coffee cake left over from yesterday?"

"Oatmeal is good for you."

She made a face.

"Why do you have it in the cupboard if you don't like it?"

"I like oatmeal cookies."

"Well, this is basically the same thing. Almost." I was guessing. I had no idea what was in an oatmeal cookie. Other than, you know, oatmeal.

I tried staring her down but gave up quickly—she was so much better at it—and got the remaining piece of coffee cake, which I'd hidden in the breadbox planning to eat it myself. As I set it down in front of her, she said, "Bev is coming by soon if you want to go out and do something."

"Like?"

"You could try to find out more about Reverend Hessel." Left unsaid was the phrase, "...and then I'll pay you."

"You were supposed to pay me after I talked to the sheriff," I pointed out.

"You didn't talk to the sheriff, though. You talked to the detective."

"What is it you expect me to find out?" She had seemed happy with the idea the murderer was a desperate meth-addict. Very happy, in fact. Why couldn't we leave it at that?

"Well, you need to find out who did it. No one's really safe until we do."

"We could just lock the doors."

"Will you stop. I shouldn't have to lock my doors. It's my God-given right to leave them open."

It took a great deal of effort, but I left that alone. An hour and a half later I was in Bellflower walking into a coffee shop called Drip.

For Northern Lower Michigan it was a very trendy place and would have been considered perfect in Los Angeles about five years ago. It had corrugated metal halfway up the walls and a sort of bamboo wallpaper above that. I could almost hear the architect's pitch about the excitement of clashing materials.

I bought a latte with regular milk, a gooey chocolate brownie, and then sat in the corner in the back. It crossed my mind that my back was to the wall since I was "investigating" a murder—again—and might already be in danger. The thought made me break out laughing all alone at my table.

Well, it was funny, wasn't it?

I'd worked my way down to a hearty chuckle when Opal walked in. I'd met Opal a few months before when she and two friends of hers offered the reward for information about Sammy Hart's killing.

She was a thick-hipped, bisexual, geeky girl with heaps of attitude. Even though she was exactly the kind of girl I avoided in Los Angeles, she'd been useful for information and rides—she had a Volkswagen beetle done up like a ladybug with spots and eyelashes on the headlights. My plan was to see if she had any information on Reverend Hessel.

Her hair, which had been orange and then purple, was now approximately an eighth of an inch long and green with yellow and orange dots here and there. She looked like a leopard. If leopards came in fluorescent colors.

Wearing a dingy raincoat—even though it wasn't raining—a black leotard, black tights and pink ballet slippers, she plunked down in front of me.

"You're going to buy me coffee, aren't you?"

I hadn't planned on buying her anything.

"Sure," I said, hoping there was enough room on my Visa for a second coffee drink.

"I want a soy latte and a lemon poppy seed muffin."

I guessed I also had to wait on her. I went back up to the

counter, told the barista what she wanted, gave him a name, paid, and tipped generously. Thankfully, the charge went through.

Back at the table I said, "Ugg, I can't tell you how nice it is to see someone my own age."

"But you don't like me."

"That doesn't mean it's not nice to see you."

"What do you want?"

"I thought it would be fun to catch up."

"No, you didn't."

"Suspicious much?"

She simply glared at me until the barista called out, "Topaz, Topaz."

"Seriously, you think that's funny?"

I did, actually. She pushed her chair back noisily and went over to the counter. She picked up her coffee and her muffin and was back in a flash.

"You got the reward, didn't you?"

"Yes, I did."

Did she want me to say thank you? I really didn't think I needed to. You don't say thank you for things you've earned.

"You shouldn't have taken it. A lot of people contributed small amounts to make that possible. I gave five hundred dollars."

"So, you would have given the money back to all those people?"

"No, but it could have gone to the Turley HIV Clinic. Sammy would have liked that."

That was messed up. They offered a reward and now she was pissed because someone collected it. What had she thought was going to happen?

"Well, the government took half of it anyway," I said. I sipped my coffee. It wasn't bad, but it was cooling off fast. "Somebody killed Reverend Hessel. My grandmother's pretty upset about it."

"Well, he was her pastor, I guess she would be."

She broke off a piece of her muffin and ate it.

"He was your pastor too, wasn't he?"

"No, he wasn't."

"But you were at that pancake supper we went to."

"I don't belong to a church, all right? I think I told you that."

Maybe she had. I had a sort of a vague memory of it.

"Is this why you wanted to see me? To talk about my religious beliefs?"

"No, I want you to tell me everyone you know who's a meth addict." I had, of course, completely rejected Nana Cole's theory of a traveling tweaker.

Opal's mouth dropped open. "What?"

"I said—"

"I heard what you said. Why do you think I know *anyone* who's a meth addict?"

"You went to high school here. You must know who the druggies are."

"Why don't you ask your buddy Ronnie Sheck?" she suggested. He was a drug dealer she'd introduced me to. See, it wasn't so far-fetched that I thought she'd know meth addicts.

"Ronnie Sheck? I've only met him once. We're not exactly buds."

"Well, he knows more about local meth addicts than I do. You should ask him."

I stared her down. "So you're really not going to tell me?"

"I don't have anything to tell you."

"How many people were in your high school graduating class?"

"Twenty-eight."

"There were twenty-eight hundred in mine, and I knew who the meth addicts were."

Okay, that was a huge exaggeration. Maybe there were

twenty-eight hundred kids in my whole school—or at least one of the schools I went to, but I think I made my point.

"Well, I guess you're just smarter than I am," she said.

I was getting nowhere. I might have to try Ronnie Sheck after all. Though I doubted he'd tell me who his clients were. I mean, drug dealers had a secrecy thing, you know, like attorneys.

"So, if you didn't go to Reverend Hessel's church then why were you at the pancake supper?"

She didn't say anything for a few moments. I could tell she didn't want to tell me. That was interesting. Finally, she said, "I'm friends with Carl Burke. I thought he might be there."

"Why did you think that?"

"Carl is Reverend Hessel's stepson. Was, I mean."

"So you know Hessel's family?"

"Yes, I just said that."

"Tell me about them."

"Did someone offer a reward I haven't heard about?"

"My grandmother is paying me."

Sort of. Maybe.

Opal studied me like I was a math problem. I could see that she'd rather not tell me anything at all but then someone would. Eventually. And it was probably better if I heard it from—

"Reverend Hessel came here about three years ago. He wasn't a reverend then. He was plain old Chris Hessel. He came from Chicago. At first, he said he had relatives in the area, but that turned out not to be true. It didn't matter though, because he'd already started ingratiating himself to everyone at the church. And Ivy Greene was already head over heels—"

"*Ivy* Greene?" I asked, a little appalled.

"Carl's mother. She didn't take her husband's name. Either time."

"You mean she *wanted* to be Ivy Greene?"

"Seriously? Your name is Milch."

"So. It doesn't mean anything."

"Yes, it does. Milch means a mammal that gives milk."

I decided not to ask how she knew something that ridiculous. Probably she learned it while giving a dairy farmer a hand job.

"Then how did Reverend Hessel become a reverend?"

"After he married Ivy Greene, he became more and more indispensable around the church. He played piano and organ, and then he was the choir director when Sue Langtree suddenly backed out. He'd give the sermon sometimes when Reverend Wilkie couldn't. So when Reverend Wilkie retired, well, it was practically unanimous that Chris Hessel take over."

"And that was how long ago?"

"Six months, maybe seven, something like that."

"You said, he told people he had family here, but he didn't. Nobody thought that was odd?"

"I already said he'd ingratiated himself. I don't know. Maybe that's not the right word. Someone brought it up once, and he said he'd never said it. He said he'd come because his family had vacationed here when he was a kid and that he'd never forgotten it. He said people must have misunderstood him. Carl remembered what he'd said, though. He *did* say he had family in the area."

"Maybe he does then."

"Or he lied. He probably lied."

"Do you have any idea why he left Chicago?"

"He said he didn't feel safe there. He called it murder city."

"Oh, well that's ironic."

Then I thought of something that would definitely get Nana Cole to give me the money. "Do you think you could help me talk to the family?"

"Ivy and Carl? No. They're very upset right now."

"Because Reverend Hessel was murdered?"

"Of course because he was murdered. What do you think?"

"They could be upset because they'd found out why he was lying about having family here."

"I have to go," she said, picking up her muffin and coffee. "I'm going to have them put this in a to-go cup."

I thought she was being rude and a little obnoxious.

"One more quick question."

"What?"

"Does Ivy Greene have a sister named Olive?"

She didn't even crack a smile at my joke. Quietly, she said, "Yes, she does. Henry *Milch*."

CHAPTER FOUR

When I got back to Nana Cole's, Bev's ancient Jeep Cherokee was speeding down the long driveway. It was narrow enough, the driveway I mean, that I had to wait out on West Shore Road until she turned toward Masons Bay and sped off without so much as a wave.

Curious. Everyone in Michigan waved. Strangers waved.

Reaching the house, I parked and went inside. One of the kitchen chairs was knocked over, two burners were on, there was food spread out on the counter. Nana Cole was walking around the kitchen collecting things, practically throwing the walker in front of her and then sort of falling into it.

"I don't think you're supposed to do it that way. You need to take smaller steps."

"Don't you start. I just got an earful from Bev."

"What did you do?"

"Fine, take her side."

"I don't know what you're fighting about so I'm not taking anyone's side."

Not entirely true. Of course, I was going to take Bev's side. Of the two of them she was the reasonable one.

"I told her that you were asking questions about Reverend Hessel's murder for me, and she told me I should stop. That it's bad for my health. I told her *she* was bad for my health and threw her out."

"You're red in the face. You should sit down."

Surprisingly, she clomped over to the table and did as I'd asked.

"What is all this?" I asked, waving a hand at the counter and stove.

"I want to make sauerkraut. You need to get me ten heads of cabbage."

"From the garden?"

"No, not from the garden. You didn't plant any, remember? Besides... if you had, they wouldn't be ready until July."

She was confusing me. "You've turned the burners on, and you don't even have the cabbages?"

"You don't cook sauerkraut. It's pickled."

I just lost all interest in sauerkraut.

"I'm trying to cook those brats you bought. What day did you buy them?"

"Yesterday."

"Oh. So they're not going bad?"

"No."

Now she was confused, putting her hands on the table as though to brace herself. They were spotted and gnarled. Honestly, getting old looked like a nightmare. I promised myself I'd avoid it.

I went over and turned the burners off. Then I opened the refrigerator and took out a casserole. Lasagna. We'd eaten half of it a few days before. I turned on the oven to heat it up.

"You have to take that back," she said, behind me.

"The lasagna?"

"The dish. Did you do what I told you?"

Oh, God—what had she told me? Something about the

casserole dishes. Was I supposed to remember who brought which dish? I should have taken notes. Crap, that's probably what she told me. Take notes.

Unfortunately, I hadn't been able to understand her at the time. That request was one of many I'd just smiled and nodded agreement to. I did sort of remember when she'd asked that.

I'd told her, "Your friends are bringing casseroles by."

She struggled with a few garbled words, one of which might have been 'dish.'

"Yes, it's very nice of them to make us food. I did check with the nurse, and they don't want me bringing food into the hospital. I'm going to freeze most of it."

Actually, that was a lie. They'd told me I could bring her food. But they'd still be charging her for her meals, and I would have had to go out and spend money on food for myself. I decided it was smarter to just freeze what I couldn't eat and save it for when she came home.

She tried to say something else. Which, looking back, was probably that I should take notes or label the dishes when I finished the casseroles.

Now I said, "I'm sorry, I tried to keep track—"

I didn't.

"It just, you know...."

She picked up a glass casserole that looked like it had been scorched, even after I cleaned it. Well, rinsed it.

"This is Bev's."

"Okay."

"This red one is Muriel Sanderson's. It's hoity-toity."

I had no idea who Muriel Sanderson was. Nor did I know a baking dish could be hoity-toity.

"This one," she said, picking up a metal sheet cake pan with a clear plastic lid. "This one belongs to the Hessels."

"Really? Are you sure?"

"Yes, I'm sure. There was a tuna casserole in there, wasn't there?"

"I guess."

"Which one of them brought it? Was it the reverend or Ivy?"

I had no clue. I would have remembered Reverend Hessel, I'd met him. And I certainly would have remembered the name Ivy Greene. On the other hand, if she'd come late in the afternoon, I might have been a little... relaxed.

Maybe I already mentioned this, but while Nana Cole was in the rehab center, I would take the occasional Oxy vacay. Late in the afternoon, when I was pretty sure I wouldn't be needed. Me time.

Maybe it's pointless, but there's this feeling I'm chasing. One I remember from being a kid. I'd get into bed at night, the sheets and blanket would be warm, cozy. I'd be on the verge of sleep, knowing the sleep would be deep and the dreams sweet, but still I'd try to stay in that spot between wakefulness and sleep. Linger there as long as I could. A delicious feeling.

I chased it in L.A. I would go out to the bars on Santa Monica, take an Oxy or two, and then have a few drinks. The right combination would get me there. I'd find that warm, cozy, safe place.

But then there were nights where I'd get greedy and have one drink too many, or take an extra Oxy and wake up the next morning, naked, in some guy's bed. God knows where, having done God knows—well, fine, I always had a pretty good idea what I'd done. Even if I couldn't exactly remember it.

"How well did you actually know Reverend Hessel?" I asked Nana Cole.

It took a moment before she answered, which struck me as odd since it wasn't exactly a difficult question. "I saw him every Sunday. And when you did what you did, he came to sit with me."

Deciding to avoid the reference to my 'doing what I did,' I asked, "Do you remember the first time you met him?"

"Well, he played the organ. I don't remember when we met, exactly. He was just there."

"Do you remember people saying he'd moved here because he had family in the area?"

"No. I don't—I think someone said he was a fudgie who liked it so much he stayed."

Fudgie was the word people used for the tourists who flooded the area every summer. Many of them liked it enough to buy second homes or even stay year-round. "Yes. I'm sure that's what happened. He fell in love with us."

"It didn't seem weird that he took over the choir and then the whole church?"

"Why does that matter? He was killed by a drug addict."

"If you're sure about that, you should pay me the money you promised me and we'll forget the whole thing."

She did her best to look confused, but I saw right through it. She deliberately changed the subject, "What's on TV tonight? Is it *America's Best Model*?"

"*America's Top Model*." I corrected her. "Yes, it is." I'd gotten her hooked on the show while she was in the rehab center, even though she'd had to start with episode three—the one where Adrianne gets food poisoning and they posed with snakes.

"Good. What are they doing?"

"I don't know. I haven't seen it yet. Getting back to—"

"The lasagna's ready," she said.

"How do you know that?"

"Can't you smell it?"

"Sure, I can smell it."

"It smells ready."

And when I opened the oven, the lasagna was bubbling hot. How did she do that?

ON FRIDAY, Rebecca Jaymes arrived shortly after we finished lunch. We'd had one session with her while Nana Cole was still in the rehab center. Dressed in a plaid short-sleeved shirt and cargo pants, she was short and boyish with a broad smile and an infectious laugh. We made some tea and sat around the kitchen table.

"Tell me how you are, Mrs. Cole," Rebecca asked. It was a much tougher question than it seemed.

After a long suspenseful pause my grandmother said, "I'm angry."

"What are you angry about?"

"I don't remember her name. The girl who was here."

"She had physical therapy the other day," I said. "She threw the girl out."

"Really? Why don't you like the physical therapist?"

"I don't know. I just don't."

"There must be more to it than that.

"The girl—she was trying to teach me how to use the walker. I know how to use the walker."

"No, she doesn't," I interjected.

She looked at me open-mouthed for a moment and then huffed.

Very kindly, Rebecca said, "I'll have a talk with them and see if we can't address some of your concerns. Now, why don't you tell me how you met your husband."

Nana Cole seemed confused, which made perfect sense to me. It was kind of a jump. I suppose it might have been a strategy, skipping around like that, I don't know. I did feel certain my grandmother was going to ask for the question to be repeated. Instead, she asked, "Which one?"

"Which one?" I asked.

Her hand flew up to her mouth and covered it. Suddenly, I

could almost see the little girl she'd once been. A cute, pig-tailed little girl, always in trouble.

"What do you mean, which one?"

It wasn't that I had some great loyalty to my grandfather, I hadn't spent that much time with him. The times I'd visited when I was younger, my mother and grandmother would fight so much that I'd get dragged back to California early. Those were the days.

No, I was just surprised that somehow no one had ever mentioned that Nana had had another husband. Picking up on my surprise, Rebecca asked, "Do you want to tell us about your first husband?"

Quickly, she shook her head.

"The cat's already out of the bag," I pointed out.

Another pause.

"He was a Marston. Will; Will Marston. His family owns the farm and feed store."

"I know it seems like I'm just being nosey," Rebecca said. "But really we're exercising your brain. Did you meet him at the feed store?"

"He would be behind the counter when my father would send me to get things for the farm. He was tall, blond, and had these light blue eyes. He was older than me—that seemed important for some reason. He'd been in the army. In Italy."

"Good," Rebecca said. "You're doing very well."

"It seemed so romantic. Like something out of a book or a movie."

My grandmother was silent. I wanted to know what happened, how the marriage ended. I was ready to yell "And..." but Rebecca looked at me and gently shook her head.

A tear might have run down Nana Cole's cheek, I couldn't tell without leaning over and gapping at her.

Finally, she said, "He beat me up. A couple of times. The last time I was going to have a baby and... I lost the baby. I couldn't hide that. How it had happened. I spent almost two weeks in the hospital. My father nearly killed him. When I got out of the hospital, Will had left."

"I'm sorry that happened to you," Rebecca said.

Nana Cole seemed to wake up, saying, "Don't be silly. It was all a very long time ago."

"And what about your second husband? Henry's grandfather?"

"Samuel Cole. He was just a boy. I'd been in school with him all along. I knew he'd never hurt me. And he never did."

"The two of you were happy?"

"Not at the beginning, no. But eventually. Eventually, yes."

"And your daughter?"

"Yes, I have a daughter."

"She was born during your second marriage."

"Yes. After a few years. After things got easier."

Then she looked at me and asked, "Why do I feel so tired? I'm just talking."

Rebecca explained, "Your brain has been damaged. Normal routes have been cut off. It's looking for new ways to get to the information I'm asking for."

"Is it important I remember everything?"

"No, that's not the point. We're teaching your brain to look for new pathways. The more you do it, the easier it becomes. Now, do you remember your first pet?"

Twenty minutes and three barn cats later, Rebecca left. I felt like I should say something to my grandmother about the fact that she'd had a husband who beat her. Something like, 'I'm sorry that happened to you.' or 'That must have been awful.'

I went with, "Do you want some ice cream?"

"Yes, that would be nice."

I took her to the ice cream stand on Main Street. She got a scoop of locally made blueberry ice cream, while I stuck to chocolate chip. I had a strange feeling, one that took me a few minutes to understand. Empathy? Affection. I was feeling affection. Could I really *like* her? No, that was not possible.

Seriously, liking her seemed to be a very bad idea, one that I hoped would pass quickly.

Like indigestion.

CHAPTER FIVE

Sunday morning, I padded downstairs still in my pajamas thinking I might make pancakes from a mix I'd bought, and found Nana Cole dressed in a tweedy skirt and a peach sweater set. That was weird. *How'd she even do it?*

I was about to grill her on that point, when she said, "Go back upstairs and get dressed."

"No, I'm going to make breakfast."

"We don't have time for breakfast. The service begins in a half an hour. I don't want to be late."

"Church?"

"Of course, church. That's what people do on Sundays."

In point of fact, it was not what *I* did on Sundays. I went to beer busts on Sundays—not to mention I'd been avoiding church for the four months I'd been there. Before her stroke, I'd simply refused to go with her. I'd only been once and that was for the pancake dinner. I wished they also had pancake breakfasts. I was hungry.

I considered refusing, since I didn't *want* to go. But that meant she couldn't go, which would lead to her doing her best to make me miserable for at least the rest of the day—if not longer.

"Okay, give me ten minutes."

"Wait," she said. "Could you zip my skirt up. I can't quite—"

Apparently, she was having issues getting her fingers to do the things she wanted. I went over and zipped the short zipper on the side of her skirt.

"Thank you," she said, clearly embarrassed she hadn't been able to do it herself.

"You did a pretty good job getting dressed by yourself," I said to be nice.

"Hurry up. I won't forgive you if we're late."

Cheswick Community Church—not to be confused with the big box store, Keswick's—was north of Masons Bay right before you got to Big Turtle Point. A small, white church from like a million years ago, it was plunked on a little hill and looked out on Lake Michigan. Behind it was a pole barn the church used for events, like the pancake dinner.

We parked and I helped Nana Cole out of the SUV, up the walk, and into the church. She was doing better with the walker—though she might just have been tired. Hard to tell.

Inside the church there were two rows of wooden pews with an aisle down the center and two narrower aisles on the sides. The walls were cream-colored, a fan hung down from the high ceiling, while six stained glass windows told Sunday school tales.

The church was only about a third full. Mostly older women sitting in ones and twos. The sticky smell of too much perfume and dusting powder was strong. Two of the women were Dolores Abbott, I think, and her daughter, Cheryl Ann. Dolores saw us and waved us over to a couple of empty spots in her pew.

"I'm so glad you're up and around," she said to Nana Cole. Then she quickly switched gears. "Cheryl Ann, you remember Henry. The two of you were going to go on a date."

Nothing could have been further from the truth.

"Have you seen Opal?" Cheryl Ann asked, as though it were a logical question.

"We had coffee yesterday." Her eyes filled with tears, and I said, "It was just coffee."

"I haven't seen her for a while."

I felt bad enough to say, "I'll tell her to call you next time I see her." As soon as the words were out of my mouth, I realized they made it seem like I was seeing Opal all the time. "Not that I see her, like, you know, much."

"Should we leave you two alone?" Dolores asked, as though Cheryl Ann and I were having an entirely different conversation.

"Mom," Cheryl Ann said. "You're being gross."

Dolores turned to my Nana Cole and said, "I don't know what to do with her. She's so emotional."

"I'm sure she'll grow out of it," Nana Cole said.

I was sure she wouldn't.

Organ music had been playing since we walked in. I didn't recognize any of it. The organ and organist sat on the right side of the church facing away from us. All I could see was a cloud of white hair. I wasn't sure, but it seemed like she was missing notes here and there. Or at least not hitting all the right ones.

Without looking closely, Nana Cole said, "Sue Langtree is back." Then she took a good look around the church. "Ivy Greene isn't here."

"You mean, Mrs. Hessel," I replied.

"Yes, that's... who I mean. And you know that."

"What about her son? Is he here?"

"No. I don't see him either."

After a beat she asked, "Do you think they blame the church?"

"I hear she's absolutely destroyed," Dolores said, jumping into our conversation. "Which is no surprise, Reverend Hessel was so marvelous."

"Yes, he was," Nana Cole said.

"Such a charismatic speaker," Dolores added. The two times I'd met him I hadn't seen any indication of that.

"Did either of you hear," she went on. "They're investigating Reverend Hessel's death as a hate crime."

"What?!" I said, a little too loud. People turned around. I lowered my voice and asked, "Why would they do that? He wasn't a minority."

"They think he was killed because he was Christian," she said.

"That's stupid," I said. My grandmother swatted my arm. "Who's they?"

"They," repeated Dolores.

"The sheriff?"

"No. He's just a pawn of the governor," she said.

That was even stupider. What did the governor have to do with it? And, to be honest, I didn't even know who the governor of Michigan was. Then, a middle-aged woman in a floral print dress got up from a few pews down and came over to us. Dolores quieted down.

Crouching, the middle-aged woman said to my grandmother, "Emma, it's so nice to see you're back."

"Thank you, Sheila. It's nice to be back."

Before they could say anything else, the organ music grew louder and the choir shuffled in. Sheila crouch-walked back to her pew. The choir began singing. It was hard to understand the words.

I studied the congregation, trying to determine if any of them might be meth heads. I mean, it seemed a much more likely possibility than a Christian hate crime. The average age of the congregation seemed to be about fifty—which is not to say that fifty-year-old church ladies can't also be meth heads, it just seemed unlikely.

Before anything even happened, my eyes began to slowly shut. I could tell I was going to have a lot of trouble staying awake. I did not consider it my fault. Yes, I'd taken an Oxy before we left, but still...

In my opinion a topic like eternal salvation is dull as dishwater. I mean, seriously, if there is a God, he put us here with sex and television and magazines and fun drugs and art and all sorts of other wonderful things. And then he wants us to think about the hereafter? I mean, what was wrong with staying here? Shouldn't the reward for good behavior be another seventy-five years? Seriously, if eternity turns out to be anything like church I plan to take a pass.

As soon as the song was over, Reverend Wilkie walked out. He was in his early seventies, trim, standing tall with a ramrod straight back. Even though he was clearly very old, he didn't look like someone who'd needed to retire. Especially from a job that probably took a solid four to six hours a week.

Under one arm, he'd tucked what looked like his personal Bible—old and scuffed with a sprung binding. He opened it on the lectern, glanced down, and began, "Today we turn to Proverbs 12:22, and I quote: 'Lying lips are an abomination to the Lord, but those who deal faithfully are his delight.'

That seems rather straightforward, doesn't it? If you lie, God hates you. If you tell the truth, God loves you. A simple message, but one that so many of us—no, all of us—have not truly heard. Think back to the last time you lied. Was it this morning? Last night? Yesterday? If you're telling yourself that you can't remember the last time you lied because it was so long ago—well, then that's a lie.

"My grandson, who is nine, would interrupt me here and ask, 'What about white lies, grandpa?' And I would tell him that a white lie is still a lie. That God does not say it's wrong to lie most of the time, he says it's wrong to lie all of the time. Lying is always wrong. So, white lies are wrong.

"There is always a way to tell the truth. If you quiet yourself and ask God, he'll show you the way."

Hmmmm, I thought being in the closet was sort of a lie.

Did God want me to come out to my grandmother? Is that how I should interpret this? Did this mean if I came out to her again and she had a second stroke and died, that it's what God wanted? Maybe God did want her dead. Though I couldn't say why. If I were God, I'd keep her down here as long as possible. She was that annoying.

Reverend Wilkie continued, though I had trouble paying attention to the rest of it. I kept drifting off. Twice Nana Cole elbowed me. The second time would leave a bruise.

He kept on talking about lying. I couldn't figure out why. I mean, I got it right off the bat. Lying was wrong. Not a challenging concept. He was basically repeating himself.

When he finally stopped, the choir sang another hymn. This one was numbered, hymn 183, and we picked up the songbooks kept in a rack on the back of the pew in front of us, flipped to the right page, and sang along.

I mouthed the words but did not sing. It was my way of being kind to the world. I had a terrible singing voice. Since she couldn't hear me, I got a few side glances from my grandmother as she screeched along to the music. I couldn't remember if I'd ever heard her sing before, so I had no idea if that was really her voice. It might have been someone nearby.

Then, a homily was read by an awkward, teenaged girl named Bekah Springer, who remained red-faced throughout. "Genesis, 38:7-10 'And Er, Judah's firstborn, was wicked in the sight of the Lord; and the Lord slew him. And Judah said onto Onan, Go in unto thy brother's wife, and marry her, and raise up seed to thy brother. And Onan knew that the seed should not be his; and it came to pass, when he went unto his brother's wife, that he spilled it on the ground, lest that he should give seed to his brother. And the thing which he did displeased the Lord: Wherfor he slew him also."

After that the collection plate was passed. I peeked around trying to figure out if anyone else's head was spinning after that homily. I mean, seriously? God slew Onan for not wanting to have a baby with his sister-in-law? And were we supposed to think that any woman, any widow, would be like, 'Hey bro-in-law, hubby's dead come knock me up?'

I've met some horny girls but, like, wow.

Nana Cole elbowed me yet again when the collection plate came by. I reached into my jeans pocket and pulled out a few coins. They made a loud, clanging noise when I dropped them onto the metal plate. People turned around and looked at me. Okay, so most of what was in the plate was paper money.

Even before the collection plate made its way completely around the church, we were up singing another hymn. Thankfully, it was not about screwing your brother's wife. Instead, it was about how loving and kind God was. I couldn't help but think it was at direct odds with the homily we'd just heard. I felt sorry for Er. What had he done that was so wicked he had to be struck dead? Wicked is such a subjective idea. He might have done almost nothing. Certainly, I'd had my wicked periods and thankfully was never smited, smoted, smote... whatever.

After the hymn ended, Reverend Wilkie invited Dottie Hamlin to come up and read the week's announcements. There would be a bake sale on Thursday to benefit the Hessel family and help with the funeral expenses.

"And wasn't that a wonderful funeral service last Tuesday! A big thank you to those of you who attended."

Then she asked that we pray for Herman Echevial—she took two tries at his name—since he had prostate cancer, Wanda Berry whose mother in Grand Rapids had had a heart attack, and Linda Geiger whose beloved cat, Caboose, had been diagnosed with the feline leukemia. When Dottie was finished, Sue Langtree stood up at the organ and turned around.

"I just want to say..."

From the reactions of people around me, I could tell this was not how things were usually done. It was also the first chance I'd gotten to really look at her. Other than the white hair, she looked to be a very healthy, strong-featured woman in her early seventies. Her skin was wrinkled but a robust looking pink.

"I just want to say how nice it is to have Reverend Wilkie back again. He should never have retired. He's too young and vibrant. Some of us have missed him very, very much."

There was a smattering of applause before Reverend Wilkie stood up again at the lectern, and said, "Thank you for coming today. Please join us for fellowship in the community center."

"Community center?" I whispered to my grandmother. "Does he mean the pole barn out back?"

"Shhhhh."

A pole barn, for the un-initiated, is a metal building sitting on a concrete slab held up with a frame of poles. Hence the name. The 'Community Center' did have several upgrades. There was indoor/outdoor wall to wall carpet with a notice-ably thin pad underneath and sheet rock on the walls, so it looked sort of like a regular room—except cheap.

The walls had been painted white and there was nothing on them except for a few scuff marks toward the bottom from moving furniture around. There wasn't even a picture of Christ.

A folding banquet table had been set up for fellowship with an industrial sized coffee pot, two trays of sugar cookies and a gigantic jug of lemonade all set out on a plastic gingham tablecloth. Scattered around the room were half a dozen folding chairs.

Most of the congregation had trickled over. I'd tried to get out of it, questioning whether Nana Cole had the energy to stay. She snapped at me, letting me know she'd be staying for fellowship even if it killed her. Then I tried to get her to sit in one of the folding chairs but that didn't work either.

Giving up, I got us both a lemonade and then asked, under

my breath, "So what was that thing Sue Langtree said all about?"

"I don't know. I thought everyone loved Reverend Hessel. He was nothing but wonderful to me."

"People liked him more than Reverend Wilkie?"

"Much more. Reverend Wilkie is sloppy, I guess you'd say. Like today. The homily should really go with the sermon. They should support each other. I don't know why he'd choose Genesis for a homily."

"Maybe the girl chose it."

"Oh she couldn't have. Didn't you see her? She was so embarrassed. Mortified, really."

"I heard Sue Langtree backed out of directing the choir suddenly."

Nana Cole nodded. "There was a rumor going around that she had cancer."

"She doesn't look like she has cancer."

"No, she doesn't."

"She seems *very* happy to be back."

She nodded.

"And *very* happy that Reverend Wilkie is back."

"Yes. That was made clear."

I was wondering what was going on there. My guess was that Reverend Hessel had something to do with them both stepping down. Was it blackmail? Was something romantic going on between the choir leader and the reverend?

"Is Reverend Wilkie married?"

"He is. Tragic story. His wife has Alls-heimers. She's in a home. Been there for years. People say he only goes to see her once a week, after the service to tell her how it went. Typical male. It's all about him."

"What do you want him to do? Talk politics?"

That earned me a sniff. Friends of hers began stopping by to tell her how well she looked and how happy they were she was getting better. I tried to smile when she introduced me but

—outside of a West Hollywood gay bar—I sort of suck at small talk.

"You should mingle," she said, under her breath. "Try to find out more about this hate crime idea."

I just shook my head. Even if I believed that theory, there's no way anyone there would be able to give me more information. I refused to mingle and stood there for another fifteen minutes. Then I remembered that one of the two offices at the far end of the room was the one Reverend Hessel was killed in. That was something I wanted to see.

Nana Cole was chatting with a woman twice her size who talked about her dog, managing to use the term 'wiener dog' about three times in each sentence. Subtly, I drifted off to the other end of the large room. Both office doors stood open, I peeked into the one on the right and found what looked like a conference room, or maybe a break room, I couldn't be sure. There was a large table in the center, a cupboard with a sink in the center, and a rolling cart that held a microwave. Not the room Reverend Hessel was killed in.

The second door opened onto an office. It smelled freshly of paint. There was a large desk, a credenza, a chair behind the desk and two chairs in front of it. Pictures and diplomas sat on the floor waiting to be hung. They were Reverend Wilkie's. He'd already moved back in.

Bludgeoned, I remembered. Did that mean Reverend Hessel bled a lot? Had the killer tried to clean it up or had someone else—

Oh crap. That's why it smelled like paint. They hadn't been able to clean the blood off the walls. They'd painted over it. Which made me wonder, *What about the clothes the killer wore?* Had they been destroyed? Or were they still floating around somewhere?

Then I noticed a cardboard box sitting behind the desk next to the credenza. Slipping all the way into the office, I could see that the box held pens and pencils, floss, a stapler, a coffee cup that read Treble Maker, a bottle of aspirin, a family photo of Hessel with a red-haired woman, and an Emo-looking teenaged boy—well, young man really, a certificate of honorable mention for a piano competition in Downers Grove, Illinois, and a photo of Ronald Reagan. There were a few things underneath I couldn't see.

I was about to do a deeper dive into the box, when someone behind me cleared their throat. I turned and there was Reverend Wilkie.

"Oh, hi," I said. "I was looking for the bathroom?"

"The bathrooms are in the church itself. On either side of the vestibule."

I thought it was cute that he thought I knew what a vestibule was. He must have read my mind—a creepy talent in a minister, if you think about it—because he added, "Just as you enter the church."

He meant the lobby. Why didn't he just say lobby? I smiled at him, saying, "Okay, I guess I'll just do that."

"I suppose you think it's inappropriate the way I've moved my things back in."

"No. Why would I—I mean, my opinion doesn't matter a whole lot, does it?"

"It was my office first, you'll recall."

"Actually, I don't recall. I mean, I just got here in February."

He looked me up and down. I considered hopping from foot to foot as though I urgently had to pee, but I didn't think he'd buy it.

"You're Emma Cole's grandson, aren't you?"

"Yes, sir."

"Judgmental. The two of you."

I opened my mouth to object—I mean he didn't know me from Adam—but then I stopped. He didn't like Nana Cole, but she seemed popular at the church. And only half the congregation applauded when Sue Langtree talked about how nice it was that he was back. So, was there a whole group who were against him? Was that part of why he retired?

"Excuse me," I said. "I'm going to go find that vestibule."

As I walked across the pole barn, Nana Cole called out for me, "Henry, come here for a second."

She was standing with Sue Langtree of all people. When I got close enough, my grandmother said to Sue, "Ask him. Go ahead."

"Do you sing?" she asked. "We're in desperate need of a tenor."

"I don't."

With a glance at Nana Cole, she asked again, "Not even a little?"

I shook my head. Nana Cole poked me in the arm.

"What?"

"He's lying," she said. "Henry has a very sweet voice. He should come sing for you. When would be a good time?"

"Oh, no, no... I cannot—"

"We have fifty dollars a week for a good tenor," Sue said.

The money was tempting, of course, but getting paid would not make me a good singer.

"How about Wednesday afternoon around three?" Sue suggested.

"I can't leave my grandmother. Her health—"

"Bring her with you," Sue said, then noticed someone across the room waving at her. "Oh God, Carla Allen. I have to hide. She wants us to do selections from *Godspell*."

And with that she was gone.

CHAPTER SIX

"What was that about?" I asked as we pulled away from the church.

"Sue Langtree knows things. I'm sure of it. Now you have an opportunity to ask her."

"I thought you decided it was an anti-Christian hate crime?"

"That's still a strong possibility. Sue is just the sort to have liberal friends."

"Nana, a lot of my friends are liberals. None of them are violent."

"Mmmm-hmmm," she said, clearly not believing me.

I rolled my eyes but decided not to continue down that very dark road.

"I think you should pay me the money you promised me."

"And I think you should actually earn it."

"I did what you asked. I talked to someone in the sheriff's office."

"Yes, well, after thinking about it, I think you need to do more. I'll pay you after you talk to Sue Langtree."

"You told her I have a very sweet voice."

"It's all right to lie for the right reasons."

"Did you not pay any attention to the sermon today?"

"Well, you might have a sweet voice. I've never heard you sing."

"Trust me, I can't sing."

"I thought as much. Your mother can't sing either."

That I knew. I don't think my mother had ever taken a shower without mangling something or other from the Whitney Houston songbook. Grudgingly, I admitted to myself that spending a little time with Sue Langtree was probably a good idea. I mean, if we were really going to figure this out.

"Reverend Wilkie doesn't like you."

"Of course he likes me. It wouldn't be Christian of him not to like me."

"You don't like him."

"I'm not a reverend. I don't have to like everybody."

"Okay, so why don't you like him?"

"He just isn't... he isn't inspiring. That's all." That sounded like code for something. Like she didn't care for his politics, or she preferred a minister who'd threaten them with hell and damnation rather than pointing out that lying is a bad thing.

"Why don't you just go to another church?"

"I've been attending Cheswick Community Church since I was a child. It's always been my church. More so than his."

"Do you think he killed Reverend Hessel to get his job back?"

"Henry, what a thing to say." I could tell she thought she should be horrified but couldn't quite pull it off. "That would be very extreme, don't you think?"

I shrugged. "In L.A. you can end up dead for just cutting someone off on the 405. Killing for a job seems almost reasonable."

We were passing by Benson's Country Store, and I remembered there was a little sandwich shop in the same complex. I turned in and parked in front of Megan's Nook and asked my grandmother what she wanted for lunch.

"We have sandwich fixings at home, don't we?"

"This is better. What kind of sandwich do you want?"

"The kind I can make in my own kitchen."

"Uh-huh. How about turkey?"

"Roast beef."

"On whole wheat?"

"Sourdough."

I was sure someone had said she should be watching her diet—i.e., avoiding red meat and white bread—but I decided to settle for getting her to eat at all. I got out of the SUV and walked into the little shop.

And by little, I mean miniscule. There were three tables, a counter where you could order, and behind that an itsy-bitsy kitchen where the sandwiches were made. Above the counter was a blackboard menu. Every item had a cutesy name. I struggled to figure it out.

The sandwich maker, a middle-aged woman with crinkled brown hair, stepped over and asked, "What'll you have?"

"I'll have the Turkey Trot." A turkey, Swiss and cranberry sauce sandwich on dark wheat. "And... do you have just roast beef on sourdough?"

"That would be the Mad Cow."

Well, that was an unfortunate name. I added a couple of red cream sodas, paid, and then waited for the crinkle-haired woman to make my sandwiches.

She decided to talk while she made them. "You're coming from church, aren't you?"

"We are," I said reluctantly.

She nodded while she laid out the bread. "I always get busy when church lets out."

I was alone in the shop. I guess I constituted a rush.

"Who gave the sermon this morning?"

"Reverend Wilkie."

"And the congregation was glad to have him back?"

"I don't know if I'd say that."

"I suppose I gave them too much credit."

"You didn't like Reverend Hessel?"

"He was cheating on his wife."

"You mean Reverend Wilkie?"

"That old man? No, I mean Reverend Hessel. He was cheating on his wife."

"How do you know that?"

"I hear things, that's all."

Well, that was inconclusive. I didn't think I could actually believe her. I mean, had she even known Reverend Hessel? I went ahead and asked, "Did you know Reverend Hessel?"

"He'd come in every so often. He liked the Corny Rube."

"...and he'd lean over the counter and say, 'by the way, I'm having an affair.'"

"A friend of his wife told me. I don't want to say more than that. I'm not a gossip."

Obviously, she *was* a gossip. She was telling me stuff and she didn't know me from Adam. She set the bag of sandwiches and sodas in front of me.

"Tell your grandmother I said, 'hey'."

Okay, so I guess she did know me from Adam. I thanked her and slipped out of the shop. At the Escalade, I opened the passenger door behind the driver and put the bag of sandwiches onto the floor since I didn't want the sodas to spill all over.

I did *not* tell my grandmother about Reverend Hessel's possible unfaithfulness. It wasn't what she wanted to hear. But what did she want to hear? The idea that her beloved reverend was killed by a burglar hadn't satisfied her. And as much as she like the idea of an anti-Christian hate crime, that wasn't exactly sticking.

So, what would? I mean, we weren't going to find out he was killed because he was such a great guy. If it wasn't a burglar—and honestly, I didn't think it was—then he had to have done something to make someone want to kill him. Most of the time that would mean he'd done something bad.

Turning the radio on, I found my regular NPR station. As I drove, I learned that the Czech Republic had voted to join the European Union, something happened or didn't happen in the Middle East, women are better than men at going without sleep, and *Sex and the City* was beginning its final season.

I adored *Sex and the City*, having spent a weekend watching the first three seasons on VHS tape (which meant I was still two seasons behind). Samantha Jones was my spirit animal.

"Can we get HBO?"

"No."

I swear, murdering my grandmother seemed like a better idea every day. I mean, I wouldn't really... but that thought brought me back to Reverend Hessel as I drove up to Nana Cole's house. Honestly, I couldn't care less who killed him. I just needed the money.

Before we went into the house, I said, "You know, it probably was a burglar who killed Reverend Hessel."

"You don't really think that, do you?"

"Why not? Yeah, there were people in his life who had a reason to kill him, but that doesn't mean they did."

"It doesn't mean they didn't either."

"Well, who would you like to have killed your minister?" I asked. It was certainly a different approach to things.

"You're not taking this seriously. You're humoring me to get the money I offered you."

Unfortunately, that was very close to the truth. Well, not close, actually the truth. Wanting to change the subject, I asked, "Have you made up with Bev?"

"I don't see where that's your business."

"In other words, no."

CHAPTER SEVEN

The following morning, I had a brilliant idea. I'd return the Hessel's casserole dish. Opal hadn't wanted to introduce me to the family, so it was perfect. I had a reason to go. Hopefully, this would satisfy my grandmother and she'd pay me. The only problem was, I didn't know what to do with her. I still wasn't supposed to leave her alone and she didn't have any physical therapy scheduled.

I thought about dropping her off at the Conservancy and asking Bev to take care of her for an hour or two, even though they hadn't made up yet. But that felt too much like a bad sitcom, 'Mooch drops his grandma off at her friend's office so the two stubborn women are forced to make up.' Laughs ensue.

In the end, I decided to just take her with me. It would look less like I was there to ask questions and more like a regular condolence visit. About eleven, I hustled Nana Cole into the car and then drove to the other side of Masons Bay, the north side, and found a road called Revolt that ran along the water. I turned onto it, continuing in a circuitous route until I found Apple Court. The Hessels lived in the third house on the left, fronting on the lake. Well, most of them lived there. Reverend Hessel didn't live anywhere anymore. He was dead.

Sitting amid a thick grove of trees, the house was built like a Swiss chalet. The bottom floor was part basement, the second floor had a deck hanging off it and the third floor was crammed up under the steeply pitched roof. The property slopped down to a neglected garden and a bit of beach.

After parking in front of the garage, we walked down a winding boardwalk toward the house, my attention focused mainly on how my grandmother was getting on with her walker.

Not well.

"Slow down, Nana," I said a couple of times. She just couldn't grasp the idea that she should take smaller steps.

A windowed-door led into the basement and, as it seemed to be the only door, I knocked on it. Nothing happened. I was about to knock again when a voice above us said, "Emma, you're out and about. And is that your grandson, Mooch?"

Looking up at the deck, I saw the woman from the picture in Reverend Hessel's box and thought, well, remembered, *Oh God. I did meet her.* Late-thirties, dyed red hair, crow's feet around her eyes and mouth, she wore a long jean skirt and a plaid blouse. I sort of, kind of, remembered her coming by and giving me a casserole. I hadn't invited her in, which I suppose was rude.

"Henry," Nana Cole said. "His name is Henry."

"Of course, Henry."

"I brought back your casserole dish," I said, my face burning from my grandmother's laser-like stare. Ivy happened to be the only person in Masons Bay who'd actually used my nickname, so I suppose I should have been nice enough to remember her.

"Oh, you didn't have to do that," she said. "I've got so many casserole dishes. You can come in, the door's open."

I opened it, as Nana Cole said, "Of course we had to bring

the casserole dish back. It's just neighborly." She looked at the dish I was holding and sighed. "Of course, we'd be better neighbors if we'd filled the dish back up."

We stepped into a laundry room and then into what appeared to be a family room. On one side, was a staircase to the upstairs. Another held a large window looking out at the lake. The deck was above that.

Nana made an awful racket on her way to sit down on an equally noisy, brown leather sectional. I sat down next to her, making my own crunch. I had already set the casserole dish onto the wet bar.

"You mean, we should have brought a casserole?" I whispered. "Why does she deserve a casserole?"

"Her husband died."

"Is that some kind of accomplishment?" I said to be obtuse.

"It's just what you do."

Now that I knew more about my grandmother, about her first abusive marriage and her second marriage not starting off well, her adherence to rules and social customs made more sense. Life could take nasty turns; she needed something to grasp onto. Well, maybe we all did.

"And stop telling people your name is Mooch. Mooch Milch? Why would you want anyone—"

Ivy Greene came down the stairs. She was smiling and looked a lot more like a contented TV mom than a bereaved widow. "It's nice to have company."

"But aren't people—" I said, and then stopped myself. We'd gotten so much from so many people when Nana nearly died. It seemed like an actual death should have swamped Ivy Greene with casseroles and condolence visits.

"Can I get you something to drink?" Ivy asked. "I've got some pop and bottled water down here." She nodded at a wet bar. "Or I could go upstairs and make tea?"

"Please don't go to any trouble," Nana said.

"It's no trouble."

"I'll have a Coke if you have one," I said.

As she walked over to the half refrigerator under the wet bar to get my soda, she kept talking. "I was so glad to hear that you're improving, Emma. We were all worried there for a bit."

"Thank you. And I'm... I didn't hear about Reverend Hessel until I got home the other day. Otherwise, I would have tried to call from... the, uh, oh what was it called..."

"Brookhaven Fields Rehabilitation Center," I supplied.

"That's a mouthful," Nana said. "No wonder I can't... remember it."

"You shouldn't worry about that," Ivy said kindly, as she handed me an unopened can of Coke. I sprung the top and took a bubbly sip.

"Well, I'm so sorry about dear Reverend Hessel. I liked him so much."

"Thank you," Ivy said.

"Was it normal for him to be at the church on a Thursday?" I asked.

"Chris devoted a great deal of his time to the church. When people needed him, he was there. That night, he told me a parishioner had called and needed guidance. That happened a lot."

"He was so kind," Nana said. "It's not surprising people needed him."

Ivy had said, 'night,' so I asked, "The murder took place in the later evening? Do you know what time?"

"We don't know exactly when Chris was killed. Sometime around nine, I'm told. It got very late, and he wasn't home. I sent Carl over to check on him around midnight."

"Was he having an affair?" I asked bluntly.

Nana Cole shot me a look that suggested she would have kicked me if she'd had better control of her feet. When I looked back to Ivy the woman had a big, confusing grin on her face.

"Oh that. I get foolish sometimes. I'd had too much wine

and voiced some concerns to someone I thought was a friend. I was wrong about my suspicions *and* the friendship. That person turned out to be an awful gossip."

Before I could ask another question, Nana said, "This is a lovely house."

"Thank you. My father built it when I was a girl. We'd come up on weekends and do construction projects. I mean, he would. I hated the place when I was a teenager, but I love it now."

"Come up from where?" Nana asked, though I didn't see how that was relevant.

"Detroit. My father worked for Ford."

"That's quite a drive for a weekend."

"It was. My younger brother and I played a lot of punch bug in the backseat."

I had no idea what that meant. Trying to get things back on course, I asked, "Do you have any idea who Reverend Hessel might have needed to guide that night?"

She shook her head. "He was very careful with people's privacy. He never told me who he was counseling."

"He didn't keep a day runner or—"

"No. The police asked me that question."

"Of course. You don't think they have any idea who he might have been meeting?"

"I don't think so. Detective Lehmann hasn't been all that forthcoming. Someone *might* have come forward. He wouldn't necessarily tell me. In fact, I'm sure he wouldn't tell me."

"Ivy," Nana Cole started. "People are saying it might have been an anti-Christian hate crime. Do you know if he'd gotten any threats?"

"I don't think so. But then there's a lot he didn't share with me."

I was about to ask if she knew any meth addicts, when she asked, "Couldn't I get you something, Emma? I still have some wonderful lemon pound cake. Honestly, I don't remember who brought it, but it's delicious."

Nana Cale started to say "No, thank you" but was interrupted by a young guy around my age sliding awkwardly down the bare wooden stairs. Both my grandmother and Ivy Greene gasped.

"Carl? Are you okay?" Ivy asked.

"Yeah, I'm fine," he said, bouncing to his feet.

Ivy sat back on the sofa, relieved. Then to us she said, "I've asked Chris a hundred times to put carpet on those stairs."

The fact that he never would hung in the air.

Carl came into the family room. He was tall and angular. In fact, he had too many angles and I felt like he might drop apart like a poorly constructed mobile. He wore a black-and-red White Stripes T-shirt, tight black jeans and a thick pair of wool socks. Shoes might have prevented his slide down the stairs. Someone ought to mention that.

"Carl, you remember Emma Cole. And this is her grandson, Henry."

"Moo—" I stopped because I was sure my grandmother would hit me.

Carl mumbled a sullen, "Hey."

"You're a friend of Opal's," I said, and as soon as I said it, I realized I had no idea what Opal's last name was. Had I never asked it? Or had I just forgotten it?

Carl grunted, "Uh-huh. Kind of."

"You're *kind of* friends?" I asked.

"They're thick as thieves," his mother translated. "Boyfriend and girlfriend in high school. They were together when... when Chris was killed."

I wondered why Opal hadn't mentioned that. Then, I asked Ivy, "And you were here, alone?"

"Oh, no. I was out. I was down at Main Street Cafe having a glass of chardonnay. I've become a bit of a regular."

"I see," I said.

"The barmaid, Eva Bailey, is a friend of mine."

"Of course. Did Reverend Hessel have family in the area? I heard a rumor that's why he came here."

"I don't remember him saying anything like that," Ivy said, looking at the coffee table in front of me. "People gossip." Then, as though remembering what she'd said earlier about her friend, added, "Well, obviously."

I looked at Carl. Opal had said he remembered Chris saying he had family here, but now, instead of correcting his mother, he was looking at the ceiling. I'd stared at enough ceilings in my time to know they were lying about this. But why? If Reverend Hessel had family in the area shouldn't the police know about that? Or did they already know?

It was obvious any relatives he had in Wyandot County weren't named Hessel. It would be too easy for people to put that together. My grandmother had this stupid sign in her downstairs bathroom that said, 'The nice part about living in Masons Bay is that if you don't know what you're doing someone else always does.'

Carl stopped looking at the ceiling and asked his mother, "Is it lunch time?"

"Soon," Ivy said. Then she looked at us and smiled.

"Well—" Nana said.

"It must have been awful," I said to Carl. "Finding your stepfather dead."

"Yeah, it sucked."

"Was he a good stepfather?"

Carl just shrugged. Ivy stepped in. "Things were challenging once he became pastor. He continued to lead the choir, so between rehearsals, ministering to parishioners, preparing his sermons, and doing the business of the church... Well, we didn't see him as much as we'd have liked."

It was quiet for a moment, then Ivy said, "You're the boy who found Sammy Hart's killer. You got a reward for that, didn't you?"

"I did."

"Well, you should know... we're not offering a reward."

"I didn't—I knew you weren't. We just came to return the dish."

"And now we need to leave," Nana said pointedly. "I'm so sorry about the reverend."

"Oh yeah, me too," I added.

"We all are," Ivy said sweetly.

CHAPTER EIGHT

We created quite the racket getting out of Ivy Greene's house, down the boardwalk and back into Nana Cole's Escalade. I'm sure the Hessels were happy when we finally got situated in the car.

Wait, were they the Hessels? Ivy's last name was Greene, she'd never changed it. And Carl's last name. Crap, I'd forgotten it. What was it? Well, whatever. I knew it wasn't Hessel.

"Why did you have to ask about Reverend Hessel having an affair? You know that's not true." Nana Cole said as I pulled out of their driveway.

"I don't know that's not true. How would I know whether he was having an affair or not? I only met him twice. Besides, what's more important is whether his wife *thinks* he was or not."

We were back on the 22 before Nana Cole said, "I have to admit, Ivy didn't seem very upset about losing her husband."

"No, she didn't, did she? Do you think she killed him?"

"No, of course... not. But they might not have been as happy as we all thought."

Obviously.

"Who do you think he was meeting that night?" I asked.

"A parishioner."

"You couldn't narrow it down? You can't think of anyone who might have been troubled?"

"It could have been anyone. People don't always talk about their troubles."

"And yet everyone knows everything about their neighbors up here."

She looked distraught. "No, it couldn't have been anyone from our church. That doesn't make any sense. In fact, I don't think it was anyone from Masons Bay. I'm sure it was someone from... somewhere else. Detroit, maybe."

"Because criminals like to vacation at this time of year?"

"Don't make fun of me. That's not kind."

It wasn't, and I knew it. I changed the subject. "Do you really believe he didn't keep a diary?"

"Why shouldn't I believe that? Why would Ivy lie?"

There were literally dozens of reasons Ivy might lie. I decided not to bring that up, and said, "But if he was as busy as she says, he'd have needed to make notes somewhere, don't you think?"

"Maybe he just had a really good memory."

"And was he really *that* busy? It doesn't take long to write a sermon," I said. I'd taken a speech class in college. I'd show up for class hungover and give a ten-minute speech I hadn't bothered to prepare for. With a little effort I could have spoken for half an hour.

"The choir," she said. "Barbara says he is—was devoted to it."

"How would she know?"

"She's a soprano."

"Oh. We should talk to her then?"

She didn't say anything for a moment. I glanced over, and saw that she looked exhausted.

I told her, "You look like you need a nap."

"I'm all right. I'll call Barbara when we get home."

I left her alone the rest of the way. When I pulled into the long driveway, Reilly emerged from behind the house and ran alongside the SUV. Fortunately, he was a big enough dog that I could see him well enough not to run over him.

Once I parked, I jumped out and ran to the back to get Nana's walker. I ran because I knew she'd open the door and try to get out on her own. I got over to the passenger side just in time to catch her as she attempted to climb down.

Reilly jumped up on both of us.

Nana Cole said something like, "Gaaa."

"Down boy."

He didn't respond to either command. In general, he was a well-behaved dog but not what you'd call well-trained. Ignoring him was usually the best strategy.

Nana grabbed the walker from me and began taking her customary giant steps.

"Slow down," I said, but she paid no attention. She was nearly into the house before I could shut the door to the Escalade.

Once inside, I got her settled at the table and began to put together some lunch. I got out the ingredients to make tuna sandwiches and a pot to heat up some canned tomato soup.

My grandmother interrupted me, saying, "I want to call Barbara."

"We can do that after lunch," I suggested.

"No. Now."

I went over to the wall phone and picked up the receiver. The cord was extra-long so I knew it would reach to the table without a problem. "What's Barbara's number?"

"616-422-89—"

"Wait, that's not right," I said. "The area code is 231."

"No, it's 616." She looked confused but then giggled. "Oh, crud. They changed it. It used to be 616."

I waked over to the nearest cabinet drawer. The one where

she kept her address book. I didn't know Barbara's last name, so, crossing my fingers, I flipped to the B's. There was a Barbara there, so I went ahead and dialed it.

As it began to ring, I handed the receiver to my grandmother. She brought it about an inch away from her ear and kept it there the entire time.

"Barbara? It's Emma."

She listened a moment, the asked, "Can you come over this afternoon?"

I went back to making sandwiches.

"Yes, three o'clock is perfect. Goodbye."

I turned around. She'd set the receiver down in front of her, so I went over and walked it back to the wall phone. Then I finished making her sandwich. I wondered if I'd done enough that she'd give me the promised thousand dollars.

I mean, I could just write myself a check. She hadn't been able to pay any bills for more than a month. If I were her, I would have let them slide. But not my Nana Cole. No, as soon as I could understand what she was saying she told me where the checkbook was and that I should pay her bills. That I should go ahead and sign her name. Apparently, it's not forgery if someone tells you to do it.

And that would be the problem with my writing myself a check. She hasn't told me to do it.

When I was finished with the sandwiches—complete with potato chips and pickles—I turned around and saw that she'd already fallen asleep in her chair. As quietly as possible, I slid her sandwich in front of her (leaving the soup to get cold on the stove) and took mine upstairs to my room.

Not that I ate it. Honestly, I wasn't that hungry; my stomach was a little off and my head had begun to ache. And... for some reason I couldn't figure out, my right eye had begun to twitch. Our bodies are such weird things. They seem to be under our control and then, well, they're just not.

Even before I got to the top of the stairs, I had my flip

phone out and had scrolled through to Opal's number. When she picked up, I said, "You didn't tell me you were with Carl the night Reverend Hessel was killed."

"You didn't ask."

"So, what did you do?"

"That's none of your business."

"What time did he come over?"

"Also, none of your business."

"You're behaving very suspiciously." I mean, she was, right? Hessel's stepson was a much better suspect than a phantom burglar or a violent Christian-hater.

"Fine. He came over around eight-thirty."

That's when I remembered that exactly when Reverend Hessel was killed was fuzzy. All I knew for certain was that he'd died Thursday night a week or so ago. Ivy had said he died around nine, but she'd also said Detective Lehmann didn't want to give her information so maybe that wasn't exactly right.

Seeming to sense my confusion, Opal supplied, "Reverend Hessel died between eight-fifty and nine-twenty."

"How do you know that?"

"Detective Lehmann called me to verify Carl's alibi. That's what he told me."

Something wasn't right about that, but I wasn't sure what exactly. It just felt wrong. It was weird that Lehmann had told her at all. *And* there was something else, too.

"What about Ivy? Did he verify her alibi?"

"I don't know. He wouldn't tell me that. You know you really shouldn't be doing this? People could get hurt," she said and then hung up.

That was odd. Why did she get upset when I challenged Ivy's alibi? Did she know something she didn't want me to know?

Since Nana Cole was sleeping, I figured I could risk one little Oxy, just to take the edge off. All right, maybe I took two.

But honestly, I wasn't getting much of a buzz on less than three, so it didn't matter.

My bedroom was last decorated when my mother was a teenager. I kept my stash stuffed in the back of a drawer in her French provincial desk. And when I say stash, I mean the lovely orange prescription bottle of the nearly thirty 10s I'd managed to save up from my biweekly visit to Dr. Blinski, who Nana Cole had insisted I see. He was a godsend.

All I had to do was remember to limp on my way into his office. I'd tell him how much my ankle still hurt, then he'd examine my nose for a moment or two.

"It's healing quite nicely," he'd said on my first visit.

"What do you mean, nicely? There's a gigantic gully where the bridge of my nose is supposed to be."

"That's where your nose hit the steering wheel and I wouldn't call it a gully, I'd call it a dimple.

He wasn't fooling me. Yes, dimples were desirable. But not between your eyes.

Still, the most important thing was that he renewed my prescription. I'd seen him four times while my grandmother was in the hospital and then the rehab center. I'd been using her money to pay his fee. In cash. As long as she didn't look too closely at how much I'd spent on groceries I'd be fine. I did 'spend' rather a lot for one person. Particularly one person who was eating a lot of donated casseroles.

After I took my Oxy, I curled up on the bed. Reilly was right there to slip in next to me. I decided to try and think through Reverend Hessel's murder. Just for amusement.

What did I know for absolute certain?

1. He was killed on a Thursday night between eight-fifty and nine twenty. Wait, did I know that for sure? It's just what Opal said. She could be lying. Or just wrong. What I absolutely knew was that he was killed between the time he left his home

and the time Carl showed up. So, approximately eight to midnight. A four-hour window, which could possibly be whittled down to a half an hour window.

2. He was hit with a blunt instrument. In the head. Wait, no one actually said he'd been hit in the head. It's just that hitting someone in the shoulder did not normally result in death. So it had to have been his head to kill him. Right? Actually, that's also what happened to Sammy Hart... It was like it was going around. Just like a flu. A bludgeoning flu.

3. Sammy Hart was killed with a fireplace poker. They don't know what was used to kill Reverend Hessel. I only know this because if they had the murder weapon Detective Lehmann would have said so.

4. He was meeting one of his parishioners. Wait, did I know that for absolute sure? Reverend Hessel might have lied to Ivy. Or, for that matter, Ivy could have been lying. Would she lie? What would she get—?

5. Carl found the body. Of course, if he killed the reverend then his mother would have a reason—

CARL. It really seemed like... it was probably Carl... for a minute there I was sure I'd just solved the murder—and then I conked out. It felt like I'd nodded off for just a second, but when I came around it was three fifteen.

Crap. I'd left my grandmother all alone for, well, for a while. I got up and hurried down the stairs. Well, maybe not hurried exactly. I mean, I got there eventually.

In the kitchen, Nana Cole sat calmly with her friend

Barbara. Barbara, who was maybe in her late sixties, looked pale and much older than the last time I'd seen her. Which was, what? Two weeks ago?

"Hello, Henry," she said. "The door was unlocked so I came in."

"Yeah, you know, it's fine."

"Of course, it's fine," Nana Cole said. "She's my friend. And it's my house."

I noticed that her plate was empty. She'd eaten the sandwich I'd made at some point. The soup was still sitting cold on the stove. I picked the plate up and set it in the sink. I'd wash it later.

"Emma says you want to talk about Reverend Hessel's death," Barbara said. "I don't think I know anything. I mean, if I did, I'd go to the police, wouldn't I?"

"Sometimes we know things we don't know we know," I said, realizing as I said it how stupid it sounded. "So, um, he was a..."

Oh my God, I was having the same kind of brain farts my grandmother had. Crap.

"You want to know if Reverend Hessel was a good choir director?" Barbara guessed.

"Yes, was he?"

"He was. He understood music. He'd obviously trained. Somewhere in Chicago, I guess. I don't remember him ever saying where."

"Did he play an instrument?"

She looked a bit confused. "He played piano and organ. Everyone knows that. That's how he started with the church."

"Did he mention if he'd been getting any threatening phone calls? Or letters?" Nana Cole asked.

"Oh my God, no," she said. "Had he? That would be awful."

Frowning, I said, "Ivy Greene says the reverend often saw parishioners in the evening. Have you heard that?"

She shook her head.

"Did you ever notice anything suspicious about the way the reverend acted?"

"God, no." She looked confused. "Why are you asking these questions? It was a robbery. A drug addict wanted to steal from the church and Reverend Hessel tried to stop him. That's what everyone's saying happened."

"What money?" I asked, perking up a bit. "How much was taken?"

"Well... no one's actually said."

"You liked Reverend Hessel?" I asked.

"Very much."

"Did anyone *not* like him?"

"Well, Sue Langtree, I suppose. It was awkward when he took over the choir. I liked them both. A lot of people felt Sue was treated unfairly. Though Chris, Reverend Hessel, really was a better..."

"How was she treated unfairly?" I asked.

"I'm not really sure. It was all a bit murky. I heard a rumor that Sue was blackmailed but that's ridiculous. You don't blackmail someone for a volunteer choir position."

"It does fit," Nana said. "Sue left very abruptly. That doesn't sound like someone who wanted to leave. And she's certainly happy to be back."

"She's back?" Barbara asked.

"Yes. You weren't in church on Sunday. Haven't you been going to choir rehearsal?"

Barbara became even paler and shook her head. My grandmother asked, "Barbara, are you okay? You don't look well."

"I, um, my grandson is missing in Iraq."

"Oh," Nana Cole said. "Barbara, you should have said." After an uncomfortable moment she added, "I'm sure they'll find him."

"And I'm sure they won't."

"But..."

"It's been over a week."

There really wasn't anything to say. Everything I thought to say seemed lame. Finally, I asked, "Barbara, why did you come here? You should be at home."

She shook her head.

"No. Doing things is better. I hope I've been able to help."

"You have," I said, though I had no idea if that was true.

"Get Barbara more tea," Nana Cole said. "With, um, maybe some whiskey in it."

CHAPTER NINE

Barbara left an hour or so later. The afternoon had gotten awfully hot, I opened all the windows and left the door standing open in hopes of a breeze. It was only seventy-five degrees, which in L.A. was super comfortable. For some reason, in Michigan it was super uncomfortable. I mean, seriously, Michigan seventy-five was like L.A. ninety.

As I sweated my way through cleaning up, I decided it was time to lower the boom on my grandmother. "I think I've done enough. You need to give me the thousand dollars you promised me."

"But I still have questions. Don't you have questions?"

I did, of course, but I really wanted that money. I mean, someday she'd get better—hopefully someday soon—and then I could leave. I wanted money to do that.

"We had a deal. All I had to do was talk to the sheriff and you'd give me a thousand dollars. I've done a lot more than that. I think it's only fair—"

"Two thousand," she said quickly. "I'll give you two thousand if you keep going until we figure out what really happened."

Tempting, but still I said, "No. I'm done." Her thousand dollars and the eight-plus I'd sent to Bank of America. That would be enough for me to buy a decent car and go home. It would have to be.

"You're not done."

"I am. I'm going upstairs until dinner. We're having left-over tuna casserole." And with that I walked out of the room and went upstairs to my room where I searched online for reasonably priced, reliable used cars.

UNFORTUNATELY, reasonably priced and reliable didn't seem to have much to do with each other. After leafing through the car ads for half an hour, I realized the reward money, all eight thousand, nine hundred and forty-two dollars was not going to buy very much.

Everything I could afford seemed to be ten years old—a 1994 Cavalier, a 1992 Olds 98, a 1993 Jeep Cherokee. Okay, the Olds 98 was out of the question. I was not a grandfather. Or a Mafia don. The Cavalier might have been okay if it were a convertible or even a coupe. But no, it was a station wagon. Grrrr. That left the Jeep Cherokee, which sounded great except for the fact it had well over two hundred thousand miles on it.

One of my semi-quasi-stepfathers was into cars. I don't remember which one, but I did pick-up a few things. Like, don't buy a used car with more than a hundred thousand miles, and never buy a Saab.

My grandmother was frosty at dinner and during television—a repeat of *7th Heaven*. Ugh. Not my cup of tea. I would have gone back upstairs, but I had to wait around to help her get ready for bed. When the show was finally over, I convinced her to go to bed early.

Since she'd gotten herself ready for church all by herself, I went to get her a glass of water while she changed into her nightgown. When I got back, after dawdling in the kitchen, she needed a little help pulling her nightgown all the way down, but otherwise she'd done a reasonable job.

She got into bed. I set her water down on the nightstand and handed her the John Grisham book she was reading. I wasn't sure how well she was doing with it. She'd been reading it since before she went into the hospital.

I said good night and turned to leave the room, but she reached out and grabbed me by the wrist. "You're not from here so you don't know. In a place like Masons Bay, we all know each other. We know each other's kids, our families, who used to have a crush on who. We do things for each other. We help out. It's not like a big city where everyone's a stranger. We can't just forget about Reverend Hessel. We have to find out what happened to him."

I have to say, I was not as moved as she wanted me to be. I mean, I was a *little* moved. Just not to the point where I was willing to say, 'Don't worry, I'll find out who killed him and I won't even take your money.' I smiled at her as best I could, said good night again, and went upstairs.

After breakfast the next morning—scrambled eggs and toast—I set Nana Cole up in front of the television and made her promise not to move for the next hour. I needed to run some errands: pick up a prescription—for her, not me, grab a few odds and ends at Benson's Country Store, and stop in at the post office.

My grandmother preferred to have her mail sent to a post office box. She'd had the mailbox removed ages ago and it now leaned up against the pole barn. The street was far enough from the house that walking down there was about as much exercise as any human needed—and more than my grandmother could generally handle.

The first two errands were easy enough since the pharmacy was next door to Benson's Country Store. Then I drove to the post office, which was minuscule—especially compared to the post office in Hollywood, which was a massive, Depression-era fortress. The Masons Bay Post Office only had two windows and a small room with the P.O. boxes. I went to my grandmother's box, 292, and opened it with her key.

I hadn't been there for a week or so and the box was crammed full. For Nana Cole there were several medical bills, the electric bill, a flyer from a food co-op, two greeting cards—which were probably get-well cards—and an opportunity to win a million dollars from Publisher's Clearing House. For me —and a big part of why everything was crammed together—there was a fat, nine-by-twelve manilla envelope.

There was a counter between two banks of boxes, so I took the mail over there. I opened the envelope that was for me and immediately saw that it was my California mail. Vinnie had sent it to me. He'd done so before, though this time there was a note on top that said, YOU OWE ME 25 BUCKS. I was a little wounded. He hadn't said hello or how are you or I miss you. No, just, you owe me money.

I flipped through my mail. Most of it was for things I didn't want; life insurance (I was only twenty-four for God's sake), new windows (I was basically homeless), an IKEA catalogue (I did want that but there wasn't an IKEA for hundreds of miles), my bank statements for February, March, April and May, several credit card bills (most of them I'd paid over the phone—well, some of them I'd paid over the phone) and... eight letters from an attorney in Fresno named Martin Nollo.

Looking at the postmarks, I put the letters in order by date. I opened them and scanned each quickly. Well, it seems I'd been taken to court over a credit card I'd kind of forgotten about. And since I hadn't shown up to defend myself—not surprising since I was thousands of miles away—a judgement was lodged against me. I owed five-thousand five hundred and thirty-seven dollars, which was the original thirty-five hundred I'd never paid plus attorney fees and court fees.

I was reassuring myself that they'd never get the money as I read the final letter, which explained they planned to garnish my bank account. That letter was dated May 23, 2003.

Frantically, I opened my bank statement to check on my balance. I'm sure I was white as a sheet. The reward check had gotten to Los Angeles but it had been immediately reduced by the five thousand five hundred and thirty-seven dollars I'd been sued for. That meant my balance was a bit more than thirty-four hundred dollars.

I felt completely robbed.

On my way home, I did some math in my head. If I agreed to keep asking questions about Reverend Hessel's death and managed to get that two thousand dollars from my grandmother, I'd have well over five thousand. That meant I could afford a not-entirely reliable car that I would have to sleep in once I got to L.A.

"Fine," I said to my grandmother after I'd given her her mail.

"Fine what?"

"Fine I'll keep asking questions for you. For two thousand dollars."

"Good."

"And—"

"What do you mean and?"

"And you have to help convince my mother to pay my hospital bill in L.A."

I took a moment and fully explained that my mother had dumped the hospital bill on me for my involuntary commitment. When I was finished, she said, "I don't know that I've ever been able to convince your mother to do anything."

"All the more reason to try. Wouldn't it be satisfying to stick her with a twenty-seven thousand-dollar bill?"

Nana Cole got quiet for a bit. I could see the wheels turning. I suspected she didn't like the fact that my mother had stuck me with such a large bill. Particularly, when she was the kind of person who had whatever she wanted, whenever she wanted it. Not that she ever had a lot of money in the bank. Her relationship with the world involved a completely different sort of currency.

"I haven't spoken to your mother in almost two weeks," she said. "I think she's on a boat."

"Yacht," I corrected. Yes, my mother said boat, but really... no one becomes incommunicado floating around in a dingy.

"All right, you win. Two thousand dollars and I'll do my best to convince your mother to pay your hospital bill."

Yes, I knew it was very unlikely she'd be able to get my mother to budge, but it was worth a try. I really didn't want to get any more of those awful phone calls from the collections department at the hospital. And I certainly didn't want them getting any ideas about garnishing my checking account.

I spent the rest of the afternoon in my room, trying to decide what I should do next regarding Reverend Hessel's murder.

Detective Lehmann seemed sure it was a meth addict who'd broken into the office. But why? Logically it could have been any kind of addict. Well, perhaps not a heroin addict. They tend not to be very ambitious. But why not crack? Why not cocaine?

And what about Carl? He was a strong possibility. Though, at the moment, I had no idea *why* he might kill his stepfather. Other than the fact that there were frequently problems with stepparents. I'd wanted to kill one or two of my official and unofficial stepfathers.

I decided to put the two ideas together and see what I got. Was Carl doing meth? Had his stepfather found out and taken the drug away from him? That would explain why it was at the crime scene. And then, Carl would have a motive—

No, that didn't exactly work because Carl would have taken his stash back if he'd killed his stepfather. And then Lehmann would have no reason to think it was a meth addict.

The only thing I knew for certain was that I needed to talk to more people. But which people?

CHAPTER TEN

"You need a haircut," Opal said when I clicked onto the call.

"How do—you can't even see me," I said. Though she was right. I desperately needed a haircut. My stylist was in West Hollywood and cost almost a hundred dollars. More than I made in a whole day as a barista, but it was worth it. I had to look good if I wanted people to buy me drinks at Rage.

"Go to Bob's. It's on Grover Street at the south end of the village. They're open until seven."

I glanced at the clock next to my bed. It was just after six, I could be there by six-thirty. Nana Cole would be happy sitting in front of Fox News. *The O'Reilly Factor* came on at eight, but I was sure I'd be back by then to change the channel. She always got a little mean after that show, so it was a good idea to distract her with something else.

Anyway, I made her a sandwich and said a quick goodbye before I rushed out to the Escalade. Clearly, Opal was giving me an important clue. Though I had no idea what exactly. It didn't matter, I did really need a haircut.

When I arrived at Bob's, I parked across the street and then walked over to the salon—er, barbershop. Oh, my God, it was a barbershop. Except, really, it didn't even look like that.

Inside there were three barber's chairs, that was true. But the walls were covered with fishing lures. And above the fishing lures, taxidermized deer heads. Well, three deer heads and one very large fish.

A sign near the cash register told me I could get a fishing license for ten dollars. Less if I was sixty-five or blind. Luckily, I was neither.

"You want a haircut?" the older of the two barbers asked.

"I do, yes," I said turning to look at him. He was in his late forties, in good shape and wore his graying hair in a George Clooney-style Caesar haircut.

"I'll be done in a minute."

His customer was a guy in his sixties in overalls and gray stubble. There was a John Deere cap sitting on the counter. I assumed it was his and wondered if it really mattered what his hair looked like.

The other barber was much younger, tall and thin, pale, with a dimple in his chin and a patch of acne on each cheek. His hair was short and spiked up with gel. He'd painted one fingernail black, a small act of rebellion.

His client could have been the brother of Mr. John Deere. They looked that much alike. The radio was playing Dr. Laura. I guess they thought they were feminists.

I sat down in what seemed to be a banquet chair. On the chair next to me was a recent copy of *Field & Stream*. I did not pick it up.

Opal must have sent me here to meet the younger barber, which kind of sucked because he wasn't going to cut my hair. But exactly why did she want me to meet him?

George Clooney's older brother was ready for me, so I got up and climbed into the barber chair. Meanwhile, he went over to the cash register and took the previous customer's money. For a moment they talked about someone named Jack, which could have been about a dozen people in my opinion.

This Jack seemed to be drinking too much as he went through a challenging divorce.

Old George Clooney said good-bye to the guy and then came over to me.

"Your turn."

I got into the barber's chair, placing my feet on the built-in step. It was a weird thing; it always was, facing forward while someone stood behind you.

"So, what'll it be?"

Since my hair was longer, we could do something with it so I said, "How about a faux hawk?"

"Oh yeah, I know what you mean. Sure."

He put a giant smock around me.

"Are you Bob?" I asked.

"You're not from around here," he said, rather than asked.

"Um, no."

"There hasn't been a Bob for twenty years."

"Oh. Okay." Even though it was the other barber I needed to be talking to, I decided to be friendly to this one. "I'm Emma Cole's grandson."

"Uh-huh, I know," he said.

How did he know? Why did he know? I'd never seen him before in my life. What was it with these people?

"I used to cut your grandfather's hair."

"That's cool. I guess."

"How are your cherries?"

"They're fine," I said, wondering how exactly were cherries supposed to be? And why did people talk about them so much?

"I cut Jasper's hair, too."

"Cool. I've only been here since February. I came out from L.A. To take care of my grandmother for a while." Yes, yes, yes, that was a lie. But then, didn't everyone lie to their hairdresser? Besides, I had the feeling he already knew most of my story.

I tried to think of something else to say but came up empty.

I mean, I wanted to find out what they knew about Reverend Hessel, but that was awkward. And besides, Opal had sent me here for the younger guy. That meant he might be a tweaker. Right? And if he was the druggie who tried to rob the church and killed the reverend—well, I probably shouldn't let him know I was onto him.

"Los Angeles is a pretty dangerous place."

"Not really," I said. "On a per capita basis there's less crime in urban areas than rural ones."

Dead silence. I wondered if he understood what per capita meant? Should I have said, 'per person'? He seemed offended. They all seemed offended. But they couldn't be offended by a crime statistic, could they? I mean it was just a fact. Not to mention my experiences in Masons Bay sort of proved my point.

Honestly, I had no clue what men talked about when they were alone. Straight men, I mean. I couldn't remember the last time I was in an all-male, all-straight place. Not that the barbershop was all-straight at that particular moment—I was there. And the tweaker I was there to meet probably—

The door opened and in walked a guy in his twenties wearing a camouflage cap and a confederate flag T-shirt. He smiled at my barber, a sweet-natured smile.

"Have a seat, Tim. Denny will be with you in a minute."

"Thanks, Joe."

So, Old George Clooney's name was Joe. And the tweaker's name was Denny. I guess if you just wait long enough information comes to you. I wondered if there was a Bob somewhere who'd named the place after himself.

Joe was chopping away at my hair. Directly above Tim's head was a pennant for the Michigan State Spartans. I debated for a moment whether that was a football or a baseball team. I guessed football. Football fans seemed to be a whole lot prouder of themselves than baseball fans.

I wondered, though, if Joe knew much about the ancient

Spartans. Homosexual warriors. Probably wouldn't believe me if I told him. Though I had no plans to tell him. 'Did you know that the ancient Spartans fought as gay couples? Do your Spartans do that too?' No, that would guarantee my haircut took a wrong turn and I was not about to risk my hair.

"Done," Denny said. His client got up and crushed his Ford hat onto his head without even looking at his haircut.

Denny took his money and put it into the cash register. As the guy waked out, he told Tim, "Come on. You're up."

Tim walked over to the chair, saying, "What's up, Denny? How you been?"

"Okay," Denny said. There was a bit of diffidence in his voice that made me think there was something between them. A not-very-good something. Like, maybe Tim had bullied Denny in grade school. Or maybe Denny didn't like confederate flags. Or hunters.

Tim began chatting happily about people they knew in common. I decided I was right that they'd gone to school together. They looked around the same age.

Abruptly, Joe told me I was finished and handed me a mirror so I could check out what he'd done. Immediately, I saw that he hadn't given me a faux hawk at all. He'd given me a Caesar—just like his own, just like George Clooney's. I wasn't happy—I mean, what? He thought this was 1993? Still, I said, "Thanks. What do I owe you?"

"Ten dollars."

Ten dollars? Ten dollars was a tip in L.A. And not a very good one. It did ease the pain of getting a haircut I didn't exactly ask for. I took out some cash, tipping him two dollars.

On my way out the door, I looked over my shoulder and gave Denny my best L.A.-dance-club-follow-me-out-to-the-smoking-area look.

Damn, if he wasn't waiting for it, too.

CHAPTER ELEVEN

There are so many differences between L.A. and Masons Bay, and a lot of them don't make much sense. As I mentioned, everyone knows your business in Masons Bay. In L.A. no one knows who you are. You could tell them you're an alien just arrived from Area 51 and a certain portion would believe you; another portion would try to turn you into a TV show.

Because everyone knows who you are in Masons Bay, stalking is basically impossible. It was almost time for the barbershop to close, so I wanted to wait around and see if Denny might talk to me. I had the feeling he would.

Problem was there were only three cars on the street besides mine. I mean, how much more obvious could I get? As a cover, I took out my cellphone, flipped it open, pretended to dial, and held it up to my ear. After a moment, I began moving my lips and occasionally gesturing.

I would have placed an actual call, but the only person I could think of to call was my friend and former roommate Vinnie. Unfortunately, since he'd begun boning his new roommate he didn't have a whole lot of time for me. Plus, I owed him twenty-five dollars and I didn't want him bringing that up.

As I faked my phone call, Tim came out of the shop with

basically the same haircut I'd been given. Like father like son apparently. He tossed his camo cap into a Chevy truck through an open window. The truck was light blue with rust around its wheel wells and a collection of bumper stickers on its tailgate. Bush/Cheney 2000, 9/11 Never Forget, Sportsmen for Bush, Rush is Right, 'Self-control beats birth control,' and 'Warning: In case of rapture this car will be unmanned.'

As he opened the door, he saw me sitting there faking my phone call. He waved at me like I was an old friend and then got into the car. I wondered what it might be like walking around and feeling like everybody liked you just because you were a decent looking white guy who believed all the right things.

I mean, yeah, I sometimes felt like that walking around a Santa Monica Boulevard gay bar, but that wasn't the whole world. In fact, it was a very small part of the world. Guys like Tim got to feel that way wherever they went.

A minute or two later he was gone, so I stopped thinking about him. Instead, I got very involved in my fake conversation. Actually, it was becoming a little intense. I was telling Vinnie how angry I was that he'd sort of, kind of dumped me. Which after he'd jumped the gun and called an ambulance on me was hard to take. Seriously, I'd been forgiving so why couldn't he be?

Joe came out of the barbershop alone. I decided it was a good time for me to listen to Vinnie make his excuses, so I said, "Mmmm-hmmm, mmmm-hmmm," until Joe got into his decade-old, brown Subaru. I waited until he drove off and then I hung up on Vinnie.

Serves him right.

Denny was the only one left in the shop. I thought about making another fake call, but what was the point? I *wanted* Denny to know I was waiting for him.

It took another five minutes before he came out of the

shop. I thought for a moment he wasn't going to notice me, and even had my hand on the horn ready to give it a little toot. But then he looked over and saw me. I mean, really, who wouldn't notice a black Escalade lurking there.

Denny walked over, a smile creeping across his face. In a low voice with a rumbling undertone—definitely not the voice he'd used inside the shop—he said, "Hey. How's it going?"

"It's going," I said. God, that was lame. But what was I supposed to say? 'I'm lurking here waiting for you so I can solve a murder and get my grandmother to give me two thousand dollars?'

He didn't say anything, just kind of watched me, like he knew what I wanted to say but wasn't going to budge until I said it. I dove in.

"Do you know where I could get some Tina?"

"You PNP?"

"I don't know what that means."

Of course, I knew what it meant. Party and Play. I'm from L.A. for God's sake. But I wanted him to explain it to me anyway. Not that it worked.

"If you know Tina then you know PNP."

He kind of had me there. "Sorry. I'm a little shy."

"You got a place?"

"I live with my grandmother," I admitted.

"Bummer. I live with my father. The guy who cut your hair."

"Yeah, I figured. You drive separate cars?" I asked, nodding toward the remaining car, a red, rusting Thunderbird from the late eighties.

"I start later in the day."

"Ah, okay."

"I guess if you can't figure out any place to go..."

I could have let it go right there, and I kind of wanted to but that felt like a mistake. Plus, he was kind of cute. He wasn't tweaking to the point of homeliness. Not like some I'd seen in

L.A. I mean, I wasn't going to do any Tina. That was gross. But there were other things I was willing to do with him.

"We have a barn," I said. "About eleven-thirty?"

"Sure. See you then."

He walked away and got into his car. He hadn't asked for my grandmother's address.

I WAS BACK HOME AROUND seven-thirty, just in time for a rerun of *Everybody Loves Raymond*. My grandmother did not appreciate my changing the channel, but what was she going to do? She had trouble getting out of the chair on her own.

At eight we watched the *Gilmore Girls*. Mostly I liked it because Nana Cole hated it.

"That girl never listens to her mother," she'd say.

"Rory? She listens to her mother all the time."

"Not *that* girl. The Lorelei girl. She shouldn't talk to her mother the way she does. And besides, this is just one long advertisement for teenage pregnancy."

"So you think Lorelei should have gotten an abortion?"

"I think no such thing. I think she should have learned to say no. She certainly says it enough to her mother."

When the *Gilmore Girls* was over, I got us each a bowl of ice cream and switched over to *America's Top Model*. It was an amazing episode. The judges criticized one of the models for being too thin even though you just knew that would *never* happen in real life. Not to mention she was not the model they sent home. So in the end, being too thin worked out just fine.

I was nervous. Very nervous. I had a guy coming over. Which was certainly different. I wasn't worried that Nana Cole would figure it out. Her bedroom was on the other side of the house from the barn, and once I got her into bed she was kind of stuck there. *If* she heard anything I could say I had to walk Reilly. And that reminded me that I actually did have to walk Reilly. His last of the day.

Right after the show ended.

During the commercial, I wondered, did I want to have sex with Denny? I mean, seriously, he's a drug addict. It hardly seemed a good idea. And just because you *can* do something doesn't mean you should. On the other hand, I'd had sex exactly once since February and I couldn't even remember it. I was used to a much more sexually adventurous lifestyle. So maybe I should. It might be fun. But would it help me figure out who killed Reverend Hessel? It would be kind of awkward to start asking questions in the middle of sex.

'Wow you're a good kisser. You know what I'm wondering? Do you think any of your druggie friends might have killed Reverend Hessel?'

Maybe it was better pillow talk.

'That was amazing. You're a super good lover. And by the way, did you kill Reverend Hessel?'

God, what if he did kill the reverend? I certainly didn't want to sleep with him then. Yuck. I mean, obviously I've slept with guys who've committed crimes. Misdemeanors. Low level felonies. I mean most people had, right? But I'd like to avoid murderers. You had to draw the line somewhere.

Nana Cole fell asleep right before the end of *America's Top Model*. When it finished, I nudged her and helped her to the bathroom—I waited outside, of course. Uck. And then to her bedroom. I got her pajamas out of the dresser and laid them on the bed. She was managing to get herself dressed just fine. As long there weren't any zippers.

By the time I got her settled it was almost eleven. I went upstairs and washed up a bit in my bathroom. I changed into a Godzilla T-shirt I'd gotten on Hollywood Boulevard and cargo shorts. I really didn't want to look like I was trying.

I took Reilly out and made sure he peed. After I let him back in and gave him a treat, I quietly slipped back out and walked across the driveway to our pole barn. To be honest, I haven't spent a lot of time in there.

As I recalled, there was an ancient tractor stored inside. One that I suspected was now gaining in value every year, as antiques do. On the far side of the barn, now in pitch darkness, was a work bench with a collection of tools hung on peg board, two stacks of tires, and a lot of farming-type tools that did things I couldn't even imagine.

Off to the left was my grandmother's red 1985 Ford F-150, which I had technically totaled when I was run off the road. The whole front end now pointed upwards. I know my grandmother wants to fight the insurance company to repair the truck, and I'm sure she'll do it as soon as she's a bit better. If they're smart, they'll just pay up.

Beyond the truck were two other vehicles: a burgundy-colored Sedan de Ville from the mid-eighties and a cream-colored Coupe de Ville from the late sixties. I mean, why trade your cars in when they can spend eternity in your pole barn.

Funny story: When I was a little kid, and my grandparents were still driving the Sedan de Ville, I thought that the Disney villainess Cruella de Vil came from the de Ville family, which I imagined to be some kind of automotive dynasty.

I was wrong.

Anyway, that night I lingered by the door of the pole barn. Since I didn't want to turn on any lights and it was so dark, I couldn't actually see any of the things I've just described. I tried not to worry too much about what I was about to do. Was I about to do anything? I mean, I could just talk to Denny. The point really was to *talk* to him. Whether I had sex with him or not was simply a side issue.

A few minutes later, I heard the sound of tires on gravel. Denny had been smart enough to turn off his headlights before he turned down our driveway. He was driving the same ancient Thunderbird I'd seen out in front of the barbershop.

He got out and gently shut the door. I thought that was very considerate of him.

Walking over to the pole barn, he pulled a cell phone out of his pocket and flipped it open. The tiny bit of light from his screen helped him to pick me out. When he did, he gave a little nod and smiled in a devilish way.

Reaching the barn, he stood very close to me and asked, "Where do you want to do this?"

"Well. In the barn."

"Yeah, I know that. On the ground?"

"Oh. Yeah. Probably not. There's, um, a couple of Cadillacs in here."

"Cool," he said, holding up his phone. It revealed the silhouettes of the two old cars. We felt our way in the dark until we got to the Sedan de Ville. I opened the back passenger door and climbed in. Denny got in behind me.

It was very dark and smelled like mildew and cigarette smoke. I'd forgotten my grandparents used to smoke. I could barely see anything. That, and the fact that I might be sitting there with a murderer made me very nervous, so I asked, "How was your evening?"

"Okay. We watched TV."

"Did you watch *America's Top Model*? I thought it was a *great* episode."

"We watched something else. I kind of don't remember what it was."

Then, abruptly, he grabbed my face. I thought he was going to kiss me but instead I felt something under my nose, a tiny spoon or something.

"Take a hit," he said.

Turning my nose to one side, hoping to not actually inhale much of anything, I sniffed hard. My plan didn't work. A lot of the meth went up my nose.

"Oh my God, it burns," I couldn't help saying.

"Is this the first time you've done Tina?"

"No." It was.

"Here, have another hit."

"Oh no, I'm fine. This is plenty."

I wasn't feeling a whole lot yet. Well, obviously I was kind of nervous about what I would be feeling.

"So, you can afford Tina just by cutting hair?" I asked.

"Most of the time. I mean, I don't do it, like, every day." I had the feeling that might be a lie. "And if you PNP the other person brings some too. Sometimes they bring all of it."

"Sorry," I said.

Apparently, I wasn't up to speed on my druggie etiquette. Except maybe I was. I had the feeling what he meant was that the pretty one didn't have to bring anything and sometimes, possibly even most of the time, he was the pretty one.

He accepted my apology by pulling me into a kiss. My heart was starting to race. I was acutely aware of Denny's hands on my arms, his lips on mine, the intense smell of his aftershave, his tongue...

I was beginning to see why people did this.

CHAPTER TWELVE

Of course, not everything that starts out well ends well. Especially when it comes to sex. To be honest, sex with Denny didn't even middle well. The problem was probably Tina. The stronger the high got, the less I cared for it. It made me jittery and nervous. My heart felt like it was running a marathon the rest of my body had not been invited to, and I may have even hyperventilated at one point—which Denny mistook for enthusiasm, offering me more meth. I turned it down. Or tried to.

Afterwards, as we were pulling up our pants, I asked him, "You heard about Reverend Hessel, right? The sheriff thinks he was killed by someone trying to get money for drugs."

I mean, that had been the whole point of asking him to meet me in the pole barn, right? Unfortunately, even in the pitch black I could tell he'd tensed up.

"I thought we were having fun."

"We were. We are," I lied.

"I don't steal."

"Okay. Well, I didn't mean you personally. Do you know—"

"I don't know people who steal."

"Okay."

"But—"

"But what?"

Now we might be getting somewhere. Unfortunately, he continued, "Well, there's all sorts of vacation homes around here. They're empty most of the time, even in the summer. If you need money, you just go in and take DVDs and CDs. Shit like that. People barely even notice."

When he left—finally—I went inside and took three Oxys just to come down. While I waited for them to take effect, I tried to figure out if I'd learned anything at all. Not much, really. I mean, some guys like to get high and have sex. I knew that already. So what had Opal wanted me to figure out? And did she know something she wasn't telling me?

I guess Denny could have been lying. He certainly seemed to know a lot about stealing for someone who didn't steal. But then, what he did know suggested he was too smart to have broken into the church at all, since there were easier pickings elsewhere. And he knew it.

Plus, I got the definite impression that between cutting hair and hooking up with guys who'd give him Tina, Denny wasn't having any trouble getting what he wanted. Which didn't mean there weren't other tweakers who weren't getting what they wanted and might not be smart enough—

The next morning, I had a wicked headache and the feeling the world was likely to end before lunch. All I really wanted to do was take a few more Oxy and spend the day locked in my room. But what I wanted even more than that was to go home to California and that meant I needed the money I'd been promised. I just had to figure out a way to get it.

I'd finally gotten around to calling and scheduling a new physical therapist who was scheduled at eleven. If I left around ten and planned to be back by one, I'd have three hours which would not be leaving Nana Cole alone for too long. At quarter to ten, I slipped out of the house. As soon as I got into the Escalade, I called Opal.

"Meet me at Cuppa Mud at ten-thirty. I want to show you my haircut." Two can play the cryptic game.

"No," she said. "Meet me at Main Street Cafe. At noon."

"Eleven-thirty."

"Whatever."

Since I had time, I went to the Masons Bay Library, which was located on Main Street in a building that had once been a lumbermill or some such. A two-story brick building, it had basically been gutted and the library built inside. Most of the books were on the first floor, because the second was largely open. A staircase behind the circulation desk rose to the second floor, which was basically a narrow balcony ringing the floor.

In addition to the circulation desk, the first floor had activity rooms, computers and rows and rows of books. At the circulation desk sat a slightly overweight guy whose name I remembered was Chad. Hanging Chad, as I'd nicknamed him.

"Hi, Henry. How are you?" he said when he noticed me.

"Oh, you remember me."

"You're hard to forget."

Was he flirting? Ick. *He didn't think I'd do a fat guy, did he? Was I looking that bad? Or desperate?*

But then I wondered, could I use it to my advantage?

Hanging Chad added, "You're on the front page of the *Eagle* today."

"Seriously?"

He pointed to the periodical area. I walked over and found the *Eagle* hanging on this weird piece of furniture with a lot of wooden dowels designed specifically to hang newspapers from —kind of like a clothes rack for periodicals. There I was on the cover accepting a large fake reward check from Sheriff Crocker. We both wore phony smiles; his was a little more polished. I needed to stop off at Benson's Country Store and buy a few copies.

Actually, there were several issues of the *Eagle* hanging there, going back three weeks. One of them had a story about Reverend Hessel's murder on the front page. There was a large picture of the minister sitting at his desk. A telephone sat at his right and an in-box was on his left. It was full of papers to be dealt with. Something sat on top of them. It took a moment to see that it was glass, a paperweight, I guess.

I picked out some of the items I'd seen in the box of Hessel's belongings. The cup that said Treble Maker, the picture of Reagan, the plaque from Downers Grove.

He looked happy. Not at all like someone who would someday be murdered at that very desk. It occurred to me that this might happen to people a lot. We cross the spot where we'll eventually die, over and over again. Did that make things better or worse?

Morbid thoughts. Possibly connected to my raging headache. I drifted back over to the circulation desk and asked Chad, "Do you have access to the Chicago papers? Like, historically?"

"Not here. I mean, not exactly. I can do a computer search. But the articles... I can't access them. There's a monthly fee and we don't—"

"Can you do a search on Chris Hessel in the Chicago papers?"

"You're trying to solve the reverend's murder," he said, excitedly. "Is there a reward? I haven't heard about one."

"No. No reward. My grandmother—" then I rolled my eyes like, you know, everyone's grandmother wanted them to solve a murder.

He nodded like he understood exactly what I meant. Then he asked, "So, the search terms should be Hessel and Chris and Christopher. Anything else?"

"Choir."

"Oh yes, that's a good idea. I have a friend at the Evanston library, just outside of Chicago. It might take a day or two."

"Okay."

I gave Hanging Chad my phone number and asked that he call me if found anything out. Then, on a hunch I asked, "Do you have any books on forensics?"

"Three sixty-three," he said with a smile. "Upstairs to your left."

After smiling back in the most noncommittal way possible, I climbed the stairs to the second floor and followed the sign to the three hundreds. There were actually a lot more books on the second floor than I'd originally thought. Still, I quickly found the forensic books. Zeroing in on the one that seemed like it would be most useful, I pulled *Forensic Pathology* off the shelf. I flipped through until I found what I wanted in the second chapter, 'Time of Death.'

There was a lot of information about how time of death was calculated, most of it vaguely disgusting. The most interesting was that you needed to take a corpse's temperature—which you could do rectally, ick, or by slicing the body open and sticking a thermometer directly into the liver, double ick.

The thing is—and this is what had been bothering me—is that Opal said Detective Lehman was asking about the time between eight-fifty and nine-twenty, and that didn't make much sense. It was too exact. In all my viewings of *CSI* they always said between eight and eleven or noon and four. It was always several hours and always began on the hour.

So why was Detective Lehmann asking about eight-fifty? Why wasn't he asking about sometime between eight and ten? That would be more in keeping with what it said in the book I was holding. I stared at the book for a moment but didn't find an answer.

Putting the book back, I went downstairs and was about to leave the library, when Hanging Chad waved me over to the circulation desk. He took a copy of the Eagle out from under the counter and said, "It's from two weeks ago."

It was the same one that had the story about Reverend Hessel on the front page. "I already looked at that one."

"Check out the last page," he said. "The Wyandot County Dispatch Blotter."

"What is that?"

"All the 9-1-1 calls."

"Oh."

I turned to the inside back page and there it was. It said:

2:50PM 05/29/03 **Animal at Large**, S. Plum Point, two calves got out overnight. Calves were located near Big Turtle Road eating grass, returned safely.

11:36PM 05/29/03 **Disorderly**, W. Mill St. Female with bottle of booze yelling at people on bike trail. Currently hiding in bushes. Black jeans/red and white shirt. Advises she will stay at her house for next 24 hours.

12:04AM **05/30/03 Body found,** Woman reports finding husband unresponsive in church office. Cheswick Community Church.

THAT WAS WEIRD. Ivy Greene said she'd sent her son, Carl, over to talk to his stepfather around midnight. And here she was calling 911 just after midnight. That raised a lot of questions. Why was she the one to make the call? Did she do it from her home or did she go over to the church? And why hadn't Carl called 911?

CHAPTER THIRTEEN

Main Street Café was two blocks down from the library between Peterson and St. Mary. Originally, it had been a two-story clapboard house with a wraparound porch. By now, it had been rehabbed enough times that it was hard to tell where the rooms had originally been. The main section of the restaurant had a bar in the center—complete with a craggy bartender and sports playing on a television—and booths around the edges.

Opal was already sitting in one on the St. Mary's side of the restaurant. I could tell something was wrong right off the bat. The dye was washing out of her hair and she hadn't done a thing about it. It looked like she might be a dishwater blonde underneath, but I wouldn't stake my life on that.

"Who cut your hair?" she asked. "It wasn't Denny."

"No, it was his father."

"You should have had Denny do it."

"Thanks. But all you said was go to Bob's."

She shrugged like it really didn't matter.

"So, I guess you know Denny?"

"Everybody knows Denny."

"And he has a little problem with—"

The waitress arrived. She was around our age, perky with pink lipstick and blonde hair.

"Hey Opal. Long time no see."

"Hi Megan," Opal said, though it sounded more like 'screw you, bitch.'

"Who's your cute friend?"

"Henry Milch. He's Emma Cole's grandson."

To Opal, Megan said, "Well, aren't you coming up in the world."

That didn't make a lot of sense. I mean, yes, my grandmother was related to several of the founding families, but that didn't *really* mean anything, did it? Opal shifted uncomfortably and asked for an Arnold Palmer. I ordered a root beer.

When Megan walked away, I asked, "What was that about?"

"We went to school together. Megan bullied me for like a decade."

I had some idea what that was like but decided not to share. I got back to business.

"Why did you want me to talk to Denny? Exactly?"

"Did you get to talk to him at all?" Opal asked.

The last thing I was going to do was tell Opal about my time with Denny in the pole barn. "A little. I hung around until he finished work."

"And?"

"He confessed to everything," I said, facetiously. "He said he killed Reverend Hessel with a bludgeon he bought on sale at Home Depot."

She rolled her eyes. "Did you ask Denny if he knew anyone who might have broken into the church?"

Well, I hadn't asked it like that.

"He said he didn't know anyone one who stole. He also pointed out that if you did want to steal something there were a whole lot of empty summer homes to rob."

"Except that it's summer," she pointed out weakly. Not

everyone with a summer home spent the whole summer there. She looked dejected, like someone had just kicked her.

Why did it matter so much to her that Denny knew, or possibly was, the killer? I could have asked her that, but my trip to the library was fresh in my mind, so I asked, "I need you to explain something. You said Detective Lehmann told you the murder happened between eight-fifty and nine-twenty. But that's not the way time of death works. It's usually a lot less specific."

"I only know that because he told Ivy and Carl. Reverend Hessel ordered a pizza at eight-fifty. He had to have been alive—"

"What? Wait a minute, you can get a pizza delivered up here?!" This was terribly exciting information. I was desperate to have food delivered.

"No, stupid. You call your order in and then go pick it up. It's ready when you get there."

"Oh."

"Anyway, they know Reverend Hessel was alive when he ordered the pizza. But then it was supposed to be picked up around nine-thirty. It's a ten-minute drive. Since Reverend Hessel never got in his car he had to have died sometime between when he made the call and when he should have gotten in the car. Eight-fifty to nine-twenty."

That made sense. Except. Well, there was something not right about what she was saying. What was it?

"And so Carl was with you..."

"From seven forty-five until about eleven."

My next question had nothing to do with Reverend Hessel's murder. "What's the deal with you and Carl?"

"What do you mean what's the deal?"

"I mean, is he your boyfriend?"

"I don't think every relationship needs to be defined."

"Well, that's a definite no." Then I said, "Ivy Greene said you were boyfriend and girlfriend in high school."

"Yeah, so what?"

"And you're still hanging out."

That made her blush, which frankly clashed with the bright green of her hair. "We have a lot in common. We're both bisexual."

I was beginning to put this story together and guessed, "You're still hot for him, aren't you?"

"We're friends."

"But he's seeing someone else?"

"There's someone. But it's not—"

"Let me get this straight, you have a crush on Carl and Cheryl Ann has a crush on you and none of you are getting laid. Is that what it means to be bisexual? Never getting what you want?"

"No, that is not—are you an idiot?"

Okay, so maybe it was a little rude. But it was logical. If you sleep with both men *and* women that should increase your chances of getting laid, not decrease them.

"I don't think I'm an idiot."

"Then don't say idiotic things."

"You do realize you're not getting laid."

"That's so typical for a gay man. Not everything is about sex."

Well, that was offensive. I said, "Hey. Just because I'm an idiot doesn't mean you get to be one."

She was wrong, of course. Everything *was* about sex. And not just for gay men, for everyone. Unless I'm mistaken, it's the basis of whole schools of psychological thought. Gay men are just more honest about it. Right?

Megan was back. I felt like she'd really dragged her feet getting our drinks. After she plunked them down in front of us, she asked, "Are you ready to order?"

"I'd like a veggie burger. No sprouts. Extra mayo. On the side," Opal ordered.

Megan frowned the whole time, then glared at me. I was

tempted to ask, 'What did I do?' I mean, a minute ago she was calling me cute.

I asked, "Are you still serving breakfast?" I hadn't had any.

"We serve breakfast all day."

"Great. I'll have an ABC omelet with cheddar."

Megan's glare turned to an icy stare, "What is that?"

"Avocado, bacon and cheese."

"Oh lord," Opal said.

"Hey, Eddie," she called out to the bartender. "He wants an avocado in his omelet."

Eddie turned away from the television and smirked. "We don't have avocados. There hasn't been an avocado in this restaurant for twenty years."

He said it as though it were an accomplishment. Like avocados were clamoring outside desperate to be served there but he'd bravely turned them away.

I ordered a bacon and cheese omelet instead. Once Megan walked away, I looked at Opal and asked, "Why do they hate avocados?"

"It's a California thing."

"They hate California?"

"A lot of people do."

"I bet they've never been there. I mean, yeah, the traffic is awful and everything's super expensive, and there are earthquakes and fires and the occasional riot—but it's absolutely the best place in the world."

"I didn't say *I* hated California, I said 'a lot of people do.' I'm not a lot of people."

After a moment or two, I said, "I'm sorry I said that thing about bisexuals not getting laid."

"Whatever," she said.

"Why did you want me to meet Denny?"

"He's a meth addict. You wanted to meet them."

"Yeah, but I don't think he tried to rob the church. He has a job, so I don't think he's broke."

"That doesn't matter if he's addicted. Do you know how much a hit of methamphetamine costs?"

"No. Do you?"

"As a matter of fact, I do. Between ten and twenty dollars."

I did some quick math in my head, or I tried to, I have to admit I was still foggy. Denny and I had done four or five hits—well, he had. I'd only done one or one and a half. So that's how much? Between forty and a hundred dollars. That's as many as ten haircuts. Provided his dad lets him keep all the money, which I seriously doubted. Even if he just did it once a week, that's still a lot of money. Maybe he did try to rob the church?

And then the fog cleared a little, and another thing that had been nagging at me suddenly popped into my head. "When we went to see Ivy, she said Detective Lehmann wasn't telling her anything. But you said he told her about the pizza."

"Okay."

"Specifically, there was someone Reverend Hessel was going to meet that night. A parishioner. We don't know if anyone's come forward."

"That's what he wouldn't tell them?"

"Yeah."

Or at least that's what Ivy said he wouldn't tell him. Now I wasn't so sure.

She shrugged. "It makes sense that he wouldn't. I mean, if someone did come forward you don't want everyone to know who the last person to see Reverend Hessel was. Especially if that person's innocent. It could ruin their reputation. You can't ruin a pizza's reputation."

"Of course you can ruin a pizza's reputation," I said. Obviously, she knew nothing about branding.

"You know what I mean," she said. "Maybe Detective Lehmann is wrong. Maybe it's not a drug addict. Who else might have killed him?"

"Well, Reverend Wilkie or Sue Langtree. He'd done them both out of jobs."

"Someone from his past," Opal suggested. "Maybe it's someone from Chicago. Maybe he had mob connections."

"Now you sound like my grandmother."

"What is *that* supposed to mean?"

Just then, Megan arrived with our lunches. My omelet was more of a scramble. I was tempted to send it back but suspected that Megan would refuse.

"I heard a rumor your friend, Carl, killed his stepfather," she said, instead of offering us catsup.

"He was with me when the murder happened," Opal said between gritted teeth.

"And, of course, you would never lie," Megan said, then spun around and walked away.

"Hmmm," I said. "In California waitresses say crazy things like, 'Enjoy your lunch.'"

"She's just jealous."

"Because she's just a waitress and you're—I never asked, what do you do for a living?"

"I work at Pastiche. It's a boutique in Masons Bay. Which you know."

All right, so it sounded vaguely familiar.

"As I was saying, she's just a waitress while you're a retail slut."

She stared me down while chewing on her veggie burger. I took a bite of my scrambled omelet. Meh.

Finally, she swallowed and said, "I have a little money. My dad's family owned a furniture company. I don't really need to work. I just do."

"You're a trust fund baby?" I said, completely shocked.

"Yeah, I guess."

Maybe I should have figured that out. She drives around in a relatively new VW Bug, and she certainly spends a lot of money getting her hair dyed. But on the other hand, she doesn't act like any of the rich people I knew in L.A.

"Why are you still here? You could live anywhere. You could live in L.A."

"It's nice here."

"Oh yeah, the people are great. They're either saying shitty things to you or killing each other."

"You have a very warped view of Masons Bay."

"One of us does, that's for sure."

We ate for a moment. I continued to wonder why she stayed and then I realized the answer was right smack in front of me. So I said, "Tell me more about Carl."

"We've just always been friends. We're both losers. I mean, that's what Megan would call us. I don't think we're losers."

I could tell she was being careful about what she said. She didn't seem to want to give everything away, which meant there was more.

"We play D&D."

"D&D?"

"Dungeons & Dragons."

"Isn't that, like, ancient?" I swear my mother talks about playing it when she was a teenager.

"It's a classic. Anyway, Carl would do anything for me."

"And you'd do anything for him."

"Except lie. If Carl killed his stepfather, I wouldn't lie for him. And he wouldn't ask me to."

Which is exactly what she would say if she *would* lie for him, right? I wondered for a second how I could verify the things she was saying?

"You were together, where?"

"He came over to my house."

"Do you live alone?"

"In the summer. I live with my mother, but she spends the summer at our cabin in the UP."

"So it was just the two of you. Did you get any phone calls?"

"Detective Lehmann asked all these same questions."

I was impressed with myself. I guess watching cop shows is the same as going to a police academy.

Megan was back. She snatched up the plates even though I wasn't exactly finished with my omelet.

"Can I get you anything else?" she asked, though her face said we shouldn't dare ask.

"No, just the check," Opal said.

Once Megan walked away, I asked, "Can I ask you a question?"

"Can you ask me a question? What do you think you've been doing for the last half hour?"

"This is a personal question."

"You asked questions about my sex life. Very judgy questions."

"Could you shut up and let me ask the question?"

"Fine."

"Megan is *really* awful. Why did you want to come here?"

"She has to wait on me. She hates that. I'm not proud of it, but it does make me happy."

CHAPTER FOURTEEN

When the check came, I divided it in half and told Opal her half was twelve twenty-seven plus tip. She laughed.

"You're buying me lunch."

"I never said I'd buy you lunch."

"When you interrogate someone over a meal you should pay for it. It's only polite." She took a ten-dollar bill out of her wallet and laid it on the table. "I'll leave the tip."

"A tip would be four dollars."

"Nothing says 'fuck you' like a really big tip."

As soon as she walked away, I took out my wallet, trying to figure out which credit card I could squeeze this onto. They were all pretty worthless. I just made the minimum payment on each of them—well, two of them. I used the money I was supposedly spending on food, which meant one of them should have enough room. But which one?

"Hi Henry, how are you doing?"

I looked up and there was Dr. Stewart. He'd been my doctor when I landed in the emergency room the night I was run off the road. He was tall—so tall—with auburn-hair, peachy skin and blue eyes the color of a Malibu sky. I said, "avahhhmmm," then cleared my throat and tried again, "I'm good. Thanks."

"You look a lot better than the last time I saw you."

"So do you. I mean. You look really good, too."

"Your ankle's healing well?"

"Yeah. My foot's still attached."

"Your nose looks good."

"Thanks. But it's not my best feature."

"It'll do."

Then the conversation died. I didn't know what to say. Dr. Stewart was one of those beautiful people you occasionally see around and they're just so perfect they belong in a movie or a magazine, and the idea that they might want to talk to you is just insane so you don't even attempt to talk to them.

Don't get me wrong, I'm pretty too. But if I'm honest, I'm mainly young. Dr. Stewart was the kind of man who would be gorgeous at any age.

"I saw your picture in the *Eagle*."

I blushed.

"You did a good thing."

"Oh, I don't know—I mean, um, thanks."

"This may sound unethical. It's not. You're no longer a patient of mine. We're just like any two guys who meet in a restaurant. Well, maybe not *any* two guys."

He was beginning to sound like me, which didn't make any sense at all. He had no reason to be nervous or weird or uncomfortable.

"Would you like to go to dinner with me?"

"Oh."

Seriously, I'd had no idea what he was working up to, but I didn't think it was that.

"Um, you mean like a date?"

"Well, no, not *like* a date. A date. Would you go on a date with me?"

I had no idea what to say. I mean, he was gorgeous, so I

wondered if my lips would even be able to form the word 'no.' I should say no. I had a lot on my plate and no intention of staying in Masons Bay any longer than I had to. So if things—

"Yeah, of course, I'll have dinner with you. I want to," I said, perhaps a bit too enthusiastically.

We exchanged phone numbers and agreed to meet in front of Elaine's Table at seven on Saturday night. Then he walked away.

As soon as I could pry my eyes off his backside, I began to wonder where I'd find someone to babysit my grandmother while I went on a date.

AS I LEFT Main Street Café, I was high as a proverbial kite— and I hadn't taken a single pill. Imagine that! I had to call someone. When I got into the Escalade, I pulled out my flip phone and pressed the button for my friend Vinnie.

"Hello, this is Vinnie," his voicemail said. "I can't come to the phone right now because I've met the man of my dreams. I know, you're probably *dying* of jealousy. Well, all I can say is... hang up and call 911."

I didn't bother to leave a message. I mean, maybe I've met the man of my dreams, too. I certainly wasn't going to compete with Vinnie about that... at least not on voicemail.

Then I decided—stupidly I suppose—to call my mother. I mean, let's face it, she'd always been more of a friend than a mother. Not even a great friend. More of a fun acquaintance. Surprisingly, she answered.

"I have a bone to pick with you," she said.

"Where are you?" I asked.

"We've docked in Santa Barbara. How could you tell that awful person from County Hospital to call *me*? What were you thinking?"

"You told them to call me. You told them I'd pay a twenty-seven-thousand-dollar bill. What were *you* thinking?"

"Well, I certainly wasn't thinking you'd pay it."

"I told him that."

"You should ask your nana."

"Or you could ask her for me."

"Oh, she wouldn't give me the time of day. Besides, you know she dotes on you."

"If she does, she waits until I leave the room."

"That's just her way."

"You could ask David for the money. I mean, he has a yacht."

"We don't call it a yacht. That's pretentious. We just call it a boat."

"The point is, he's rich. Isn't he?"

"Just because he's rich doesn't mean he should pay your hospital bill."

"You had me committed against—"

"Oh please, let's not have this conversation again."

"And now you expect me to pay for what you did."

"I don't expect you to pay for it. At least not the whole thing. Did you try negotiating? They'll probably take ten thousand."

That's when I realized she knew; she knew I'd gotten a reward. Obviously, she didn't know they'd taken taxes out, but still. Nor did she know I'd had my bank account garnished. She thought I had fifteen thousand dollars and wanted me to give it to the hospital. What was wrong with her?

"I can't give them my money. I need a car—a car that I can drive cross-country. I'll need car insurance, a security deposit for an apartment in L.A., and I'll need money to live on until I get a job."

"Oh, look at you, being all responsible."

"No thanks to you."

"Oh, I don't think that's fair. You're still here, aren't you?"

"That's the bar? That I survived?"

She got quiet for a moment, then said, "Fine. I'll talk to your grandmother about paying the bill for you. Does that help?"

"It does."

If nothing else, I had the pleasure of imagining their conversation. After I solved the murder, Nana Cole would try to talk my mother into paying the bill. In the meantime, my mother would attempt to talk Nana Cole into paying the bill. Priceless.

She launched into a long explanation of David's business, which had something to do with weather futures. That elicited a 'huh?' from me, so she launched into an explanation of what exactly a weather future was. It had something to do with farmers hedging their bets against bad weather.

"He's let me pick a few," my mother said. "I'm good at it."

"It sounds like gambling. Why not just go to Las Vegas?"

"Life itself is a gamble. Haven't you learned that yet?"

Had I learned that? I wasn't sure. I certainly felt like I'd been on the losing side of a few too many bets. But—

"Oh. I have to go. David needs me. We're shoving off. I'll call Mother in a week or two, I promise."

Then she hung up on me. And I'd never had the chance to tell her I had a date with a hot, a very hot, doctor. Now I wasn't even sure I wanted to. During the conversation, I'd been angry, hurt, triumphant, insulted, manipulated, and outright confused. All of which was typical for a five-minute chat with my mother.

Before I left the village to go home, I decided I'd stop at the Conservancy and talk to Bev. If I was going on a date Saturday night, I'd need someone to babysit (grandma sit?) my Nana Cole. I wondered if they'd made up.

The Wyandot Land Conservancy office was also on Main Street; well, sort of. It was actually on the back side of an old gray house that had been split up into offices. Basically, it was a tiny room that looked out on the parking lot in the back. Also in the building was a bookstore, Village Books, and a hairdresser, Hair Flare.

I drove down the alley and squeezed the Escalade into a parking space that was much too small. I did my best not to ding the car next to me when I opened the door. I can't say I was successful.

Ignoring that, I let myself into the Conservancy's office. Bev Jenkins was in her late fifties, with steel gray hair and sharp features. She was not thin but not overweight. Square would be the best way to describe her.

When she looked up and saw me, she said, "Oh thank God. You're back."

"I'm not back. Sorry."

"Oh, okay."

"I'm wondering if you could hang out with my grandmother on Saturday night. I have plans."

She raised an eyebrow at me but didn't say anything.

"Emma's not very happy with me right now."

"She'll have to get over that."

She frowned at me for a moment but then seemed to have an idea.

"I'll trade."

"Trade what?"

"We need to staff our annual plant sale. We need at least eight people, preferably ten."

"How much are you paying?"

"It's volunteer."

"Oh. Well, I don't exactly know ten people."

She pushed forward a tin box that held three by five cards. "These are people who've volunteered in the past. All you have to do is make calls until you fill two eight-hour shifts. July 11th and 12th. Friday and Saturday. Eight to four both days."

Honestly, I felt like I was getting the short end of the stick. But what else could I do?

CHAPTER FIFTEEN

Gay men love divas. Britney Spears, Mariah Carey, Barbra Streisand, Whitney Houston. I'm old school. I love Cher. Which is why I chose to sing "Believe" when my grandmother and I went to audition for Sue Langtree and the church's choir.

Now, I should explain why I chose that particular song. As much as I adore Cher, she really only has one good note. Wisely, she makes sure it's in everything she sings. I know this sounds like I'm putting her down, but I'm not. It's a really, really good note. Unfortunately, I have not found my good note.

Once we were inside the church for the audition, I went to stand to the side of the altar next to the organ. Sue was at the organ. For some reason that made no sense to me, she didn't have the sheet music for "Believe." I mean, maybe it wasn't *exactly* religious, but it was close enough. Other than 'I believe' it barely had lyrics. I didn't see why you *wouldn't* sing it in church.

Well, to each his own.

Nana Cole sat in the first pew next to Bekah Springer, the girl who told the scintillating story of Onan, who turned out to also be Sue Langtree's granddaughter. Bekah, not Onan.

I hadn't sung for very long before Sue stopped me by saying, "Oh my. Well, first of all, you're a baritone, not a tenor. But that's fine. We could use another baritone. Why don't we start with scales."

She began picking out notes on the organ. I'd do my best to hit them, and she'd say, "Lower. No, lower. Lower still."

Honestly, it was very confusing. After I'd failed to hit at least a dozen notes, she asked, "Can you come to our rehearsals on Tuesday nights?"

"What? You're kidding."

"We're short on men. I need you desperately."

"But I can't sing."

"Don't worry, we'll work around that."

I looked over to my grandmother for help, but she just sat there. Useless. I cleared my throat and that got her attention.

"Sue, I wonder if you could help me to the ladies room?"

"Oh, of course, I can."

My grandmother stood up and clasped both sides of the walker. She started down the aisle while Sue returned her sheet music to the organ bench—which she flipped up to reveal a convenient spot to keep music—and then scurried after Nana Cole.

Bekah watched them leave, and the minute they were gone rushed over to me. "You're from Beverly Hills, aren't you?"

"L.A.," I corrected.

"Same difference, right? I mean, my favorite show in the world is *Beverly Hills, 90210*. We have the whole show on tape. I watch it all the time. It's just like that, isn't it?"

I think I'd watched one episode when it was on TV and turned it off because it was so stupid, but I said, "Yeah. That's what it's like, pretty much."

"Oh, God, you're so lucky! I mean, you were. Now you're here; that's not lucky at all."

"No, it's not."

"I bet you can't wait to go back."

I nodded. I didn't really want to talk about me. Actually, I kind of did, but that wouldn't get me any closer to going home. And this conversation was making me homesick.

"So, I guess you're close to your grandmother?" I asked her.

"I stay with her a lot. It's better than being with my mom. Not that my mom is horrible, but she's married to this guy— Steve. He and I don't really... I mean, he's a total Brenda, if you know what I mean."

I was pretty sure Brenda was a character on *Beverly Hills, 90210* and not a nice one, so I nodded sympathetically.

"As soon as I turn eighteen, I'm moving to Beverly Hills."

"Do you have a lot of money?"

It seemed a practical question.

"Well, I mean, I'm saving up. Maybe I could sleep on your couch when I get there. I mean, no funny business."

"I'm gay."

She gasped. "Oh my God. We could be *Will & Grace!*"

I liked TV, but seriously, this girl? Did she do anything else? Since Sue and Nana Cole could be back any moment, I cut to the chase, and said, "Tell me the truth, is your grandmother having an affair with Reverend Wilkie?"

"What? No..." she said, giggling. "Why would you ask that? Are you crazy?"

"I get the impression Reverend Hessel had something on them that he used to advance himself in the church."

She stopped smiling and was suddenly visibly upset. She looked over her shoulder, then whispered, "Does everyone think that?"

I couldn't speak for everyone, but I nodded anyway.

"Oh my God, this all my fault."

Something awful occurred to me. "You aren't having an affair with Reverend Wilkie, are you?"

"Yuck! No. Gawd!"

"My thoughts exactly. So, what exactly is all your fault?"

She thought for a moment, then said, "I got pregnant, and they helped me."

"They helped you..."

"Not be pregnant. They took me to Grand Rapids so that no one would recognize us."

"And this is a church that's against women... not being pregnant?"

She nodded.

Stupid question, I know. Sometimes it seemed like the whole reason for churches to exist was to punish women who had unwanted pregnancies. Well, that and to condemn homosexuality.

"Do you have a boyfriend?"

She shook her head.

"No. I went to a party." She stopped as though she'd explained the whole thing. I waited. Then she began again, almost whispering. "I wanted to have sex; I did. I wanted to lose my virginity. Like those boys in that movie."

"*American Pie?*"

"Yeah, that one. Anyway, I was flirting with Jason Marks most of the night. He's *really* hot. I thought something might happen. It was a sleepover. Nobody's parents knew there were boys there. It was a big secret."

She stopped, seemed to consider what to say next, then, "Melody Sheck's sister got us mandarin-flavored vodka. Everyone was kind of drunk. I kind of fell asleep behind this sofa. In the middle of the night, someone got on top of me. I thought it was Jason at first, and that was kind of okay, but then I realized it was this other guy, Donny Hyslip, and... he's not, um, I don't think he's hot. So, I didn't want to—but I felt bad about that, you know, not liking him just because he's ugly. And, you know, I kind of just lay there and let it happen."

She was quiet for a long moment, then she said, "My grandmother says I was raped. I mean, I guess, maybe. Anyway, that's why she and Reverend Wilkie helped me."

"It would have been okay to say no," I said, even though I wasn't especially good at saying no myself.

"I don't know. There were people around and I didn't want anyone to know it was happening. I mean, it was awful enough."

"You told Reverend Hessel?"

"I did. I mean, most of the time I don't want to talk about it at all. And every once and a while it's like all I can talk about. Does that make sense?"

"Totally," I said.

"I probably shouldn't be talking to you about it either."

"It's all right. Since I'm from California. Most people here don't believe anything I say anyway."

And I certainly wasn't going to use the information to blackmail Sue Langtree and Reverend Wilkie. And it was good to know that Donny Hyslip was a dick in case I ever ran into him.

"I mean, I am glad there won't be a little Donny Hyslip running around," she said. "That would have been awful. Looking at that face the rest of my life."

I nodded agreement. The homily she'd read was beginning to make more sense. Bekah must have identified with Er's wife. There she was waiting for her naughty husband/hot crush to come home and give her a toss, but instead she gets her brother-in-law/ugly guy who immediately announced his devotion to coitus interruptus—or in Bekah's case, not.

When Nana Cole and Sue came back in, I said we should probably get going. Sue made me promise twice to come to the next rehearsal. I promised I would, though I had no plans to show up. I mean, promising seemed like the only way she'd ever let us leave. As we drove home, I asked, "What did Sue have to say for herself?"

"Nothing really. I tried to get her to talk about Reverend Wilkie, but she wouldn't say anything other than he's a good man."

Even though he clearly didn't like me, I said, "He might be a good man."

He did go out of his way and against his religion to help a teenager in trouble. That's what good men do. Right?

"The whole thing was humiliating," my grandmother continued. "She tried to take my pants down for me."

"You did ask for her help."

"Yes, but she didn't even—well, I told her I just wanted her to come in case I took a fall. She left me alone after that."

Gray clouds hung over Lake Michigan. They looked like someone had pulled the stuffing out of a bunch of teddy bears. A lot of teddy bears.

"Sue and the good reverend were definitely not having an affair," I said.

"How do you know?"

"Bekah told me."

"How does she know?"

"Because she knows what really happened."

"Which is?"

"I don't think I should tell you."

"What do you mean? I'm paying you."

"Well, you haven't paid me yet. Besides, it I don't think it has anything to do with Reverend Hessel's murder. And it would just hurt people."

"When did you start caring about other people?"

That was such a mean thing to say it deserved a mean answer, so I said, "Last Tuesday at three twenty-three in the afternoon. You were napping."

"You're such an odd child," she said under her breath.

We drove in silence for a mile or two. Finally, I said, "Why aren't you in the choir?"

"I can't sing a note. Where do you think you get it from?"

"This audition was just to humiliate me, wasn't it?"

"No. We needed to find out what's going on between Sue

and Reverend Wilkie. And apparently, we did. You just won't tell me."

"They're not having an affair. Do you really need to know more than that?"

"But they still have a motive, don't they?"

And I had to admit they did. A big one.

CHAPTER SIXTEEN

Yes, I knew it was entirely possible that Reverend Wilkie and
Sue Langtree had something to do with Reverend Hessel's
death. Except, right away, I was sure they didn't. And it wasn't
because they did something kind for a teenage girl. It was
because Detective Lehmann thought the murder was the
result of a robbery gone wrong. A robbery committed by a
meth addict. Not a generic drug addict, a specific drug addict:
a meth addict. A tweaker. A cranker. A meth head.

I couldn't see what that had to do with Reverend Wilkie or
Sue Langtree. I didn't see how two people that old would even
know anything about Tina.

Consequently, having reached a dead end, I didn't do
much the next day. Friday. Well, that's not completely true. I
took care of my grandmother, I spent a lot of time calling
people trying to get them to volunteer for the plant sale, and I
took an Oxy vacay in the afternoon by telling Nana Cole I was
desperate for a nap and making her promise to stay out of the
kitchen.

Finding volunteers was a nightmare. I got three people to
commit to Friday and two for Saturday which meant I was
nowhere near finished calling up strangers and asking them to

do something for absolutely free. I mean, the people I was calling were all people who'd volunteered before, so that should have made things easier. Should have, but didn't.

In fact, I think it made it harder. One woman barely let me finish asking before she said, "No. Absolutely not. Last year you promised I wouldn't have to move anything. Not a thing. I spent the whole day moving ten-foot trees."

"This is a seedling sale," I replied, though for all I knew there were ten-foot seedlings. Some of the trees around here did get very big.

Early Saturday evening, Nana Cole and I were watching *9&10 News*—Prince William had just turned twenty-one—when there was a knock at the back door.

As I got up, I said to her, "Be nice."

"What do you mean be nice? Who's here?"

Ignoring her, I went to the back door and let Bev in. Despite it being summer, she wore a gray cardigan over a flannel shirt. She carried a casserole in her hands.

"It's sort of a chicken cordon bleu. With noodles."

"Sounds great. She's in the living room."

"Who is it?" Nana Cole yelled from the other room.

"It's Bev!" her friend yelled back.

"Thank you for doing this," I said.

Bev went into the living room while I set the casserole on the stove. I turned the oven up to three-fifty, assuming that they'd want some chicken casserole later. Knowing this was a possibility—and that I'd be going out to have dinner—I'd served us each a small salad for dinner. Mostly I'd moved my lettuce leaves around the plate.

There were a few rumblings from the living room, so I decided I'd better get in there.

"Your hair looks awful." Bev said to my grandmother, because it did. "How about we wash it."

I could tell Nana Cole wanted to say no and throw her out, but I'd been refusing to wash her hair for most of the week.

Bev continued, "I'm sorry I upset you. You know I only said what I said because I'm concerned about you."

"I don't like people sticking their noses in."

"That's what friends do, Emma. They stick their noses in."

Nana Cole snorted, and said, "Then you must the best friend on the planet."

"I'll take that as a compliment."

"I didn't mean—"

"I think you've said enough. Let's get you into the bathroom so we can wash that mop."

Ten minutes later, I was getting out of the Escalade across the street from Elaine's Table. I'd never been before. I had driven by the charming, baby blue clapboard house that—like Main Street Café—had been converted into a restaurant, but I'd never thought about going there. It was a farm-to-table restaurant, which I had to guess meant they bought things directly from local farmers. Not sure why that was a good thing, but apparently it's something to brag about.

I arrived first and was seated at a table on what was once the wrap around porch. It had a postcard view of Masons Bay's Main Street, which made the town look exactly like the kind of place city dwellers dreamed of after an hour and a half commute. To me, though, it looked like something out of Stephen King, and I would not have been all that shocked to see vampires, werewolves or zombies stumbling down the street.

The waiter, who looked to be in his forties, was balding on top with a ratty little ponytail in the back. I was sure ponytails were out of fashion but worried a bit that they might have come back—in which case, ick!

He offered to get me a glass of wine, but after looking at the menu I declined. The wine was expensive and I didn't want to spend a lot of money. I also wasn't sure if Dr. Stewart was treating me or if we were going dutch. I hoped we weren't going dutch but had to face the very real possibility that we might be.

There's a weird kind of structure to gay dating. I did often go out with guys Dr. Stewart's age, and they were almost always as successful as he was. None of them were ever as attractive as he was though. With an older, successful but unattractive guy, I knew without a doubt that he was picking up the bill. With Dr. Stewart—so good-looking—I had no idea. What I did know was that if we went out together in West Hollywood and competed to see who would get bought more drinks, I would lose. Big time.

For those reasons, I might be paying for dinner. Or at least my half.

He walked into the restaurant about twenty minutes late. "I'm so sorry," he said as he sat down. "My shift ran over and then, well, I had to go home and clean up. You know, I wanted to put my best foot forward."

Wow. He wanted to put his best foot forward for me. That was weird to think about. Maybe I *was* paying for dinner.

"You know, I don't know your first name," I said.

"Edward."

"Do you like Ed, Eddie, Ted, Ward?"

"Edward is fine. What about you? Hank or Henry?"

"I like Mooch."

"Do you? I suspect there's a story there."

"Not really. It's just what kids called me in school."

"The nice kids or the bullies?"

"Just kids."

He looked at me, a bit concerned, and said, "I think I'll go with Henry."

"Okay," I said. Henry hadn't actually been a choice. It never was. I didn't like it, but apparently everyone else did. The waiter came over again and asked Edward if he'd like something to drink.

"Should we get a bottle of wine?" Edward asked me.

"Oh, um—"

"We'll have a bottle of the Wyandot Cellars Cab Franc," he said with confidence.

The waiter hung around for a moment and told us the specials. Edward added an order of popcorn perch as an appetizer. After the waiter walked away, Edward asked, "So, *Henry*, how did you end up here?"

I considered being cute and saying I drove from my grandmother's house, but I knew that's not what he meant.

I said, "I came out from L.A. to take care of my grandmother."

Yes, I know, that was a total lie. But I was hardly going to tell him I'd taken one Oxy too many and ended up in the psych ward. That was not first date chit-chat. In fact, I'm not sure I'd tell a man as sexy as Dr. Edward Stewart something like that until our twenty-fifth or thirtieth anniversary.

"You're here for good then," he said.

"Oh God no! I'm moving back to L.A. Soon, I hope."

"Oh, I see." He seemed genuinely disappointed. Which was weird. "Someone else is going to take care of your grandmother?"

"No. She'll be able to take care of herself."

"But she recently had a stroke?"

"Yeah. She's getting better."

"Well, that's good."

I suspected he was doing math in his head, asking himself why I came to take care of my grandmother months before she had the stroke and why I was going to now be able to leave. I smiled in hopes of distracting him from tiny little details.

"Why don't you tell me what you plan to do when you get back to Los Angeles," he said.

Crap. What *did* I plan to do? I hadn't thought much beyond getting back there. Would I go back to being a barista and hustling drinks at Rage? I probably would, but it sounded super lame. I needed to be more ambitious than that. I mean, he's a doctor, which was like the definition of ambitious. And ambitious people didn't really like un-ambitious people, right?

"Oh, you know, I have a degree in communications. UCLA," I said.

"Oh, good school," he said. And that was exactly why I mentioned it.

"I might look for something in the entertainment industry."

Of course, I'd already done that. Most of what was available to me were unpaid internships and desk jobs that paid worse than being a barista. I mean, the only step-up I could imagine would be waiting tables in a decent restaurant. And that would be my life for, like, forever.

"Maybe I'll go to grad school," I said, though it was certainly news to me.

"And what would you study?"

"Film?" You know, something steady to keep me from that dreaded waiter's job.

"Production?" he asked.

I shook my head. "Theory." I was, after all, very good at watching movies. Though, I really had no idea where I'd find a job doing that. But then graduate school might answer that question.

"I like an ambitious man," he said. I almost jumped out of my chair. I was right to make up an ambition. Then he said, "I hear Central Michigan University has a very good film theory program."

Why would he know something like that?

"I did my undergrad there," he said, answering my unasked but mentally shouted question. Gazing into his beautiful face, I couldn't help but think that if I saw him for any length of time, I was going to have to go to graduate school just to keep his interest.

"Where is Central Michigan University?"

"Mt. Pleasant?"

"And where—"

"Near Midland."

"In Texas?"

He chuckled. "No, Midland, Michigan. It's about a two-hour drive from here."

The waiter came with the wine. He poured a tiny bit into Edward's glass. He tasted it and said it was fine. The waiter poured wine for both of us and asked if we'd like to order. Edward told him 'in a bit' and the waiter went away.

I sipped my wine. It was very good. Sweet and peppery all at once.

"I have a confession to make," he said. That was terrifying. If he made a confession, would he expect one in return? I had no intention of admitting anything.

"I went to Keck School of Medicine at USC."

"Oh, so you're the enemy," I said, referring to the cross-town rivalry.

"I never really bought into that."

"Oh, me either. It's a sports thing, isn't it?" Of course, for four years no one could say USC around me without my saying, 'Oh, the University for Spoiled Children.' But we'll let that pass for now.

"Did you like L.A.?" I asked.

"I wouldn't say I got to see a lot of it. Medical school is intense."

I knew that, of course, having gone directly from *Doogie Howser, M.D.* to *ER.* I wished we'd met in Los Angeles. I mean, we were there at the same—

"How old are you?"

"Thirty-one."

"And when were you in Los Angeles?"

"From ninety-four to nine-eight."

"It's too bad we didn't meet. I mean, not right away, that wouldn't have been legal. I was legal the last year you were there."

"I couldn't have given you the attention you deserve."

I deserved attention. What a fabulous idea.

The waiter came back with the popcorn perch and asked if we were ready to order. Edward said we were and then proceeded to order, while I fantasized about the kind of attention I deserved. Edward ordered a filet of sole cooked in butter. Then it was my turn. I'd paid zero attention to the menu.

"I'll have a steak."

"New York or filet mignon?"

"The New York, probably."

"He'll have the filet," Edward said.

It was the more expensive cut. He rightly assumed that's why I didn't order it. And that made me nervous. Could he see right through me? Was I that obviously broke?

I actually had a great deal of experience dining in fine restaurants. There came a point in all my mother's relationships, and possible relationships, when I had to be introduced. On the drive to some of the best restaurants in Los Angeles she would coach me.

"Don't order the most expensive thing on the menu, he'll think we're gold diggers. And don't order the cheapest thing on the menu, we'll look like we have no self-confidence. Order something in the middle. And order something exotic. A piece of unusual fish or something with a foreign name. It makes you seem more interesting."

I always ordered a medium-priced steak. Since she didn't exactly cook, it was exotic to me. Sometimes her dates did everything they could to impress me and sometimes they seemed very annoyed I was there at all. Not unlike my own dating life.

The waiter went away, and we were uncomfortably alone. I tried the popcorn perch. It was yummy. Since I was already thinking of my mother, I wondered what she would do in this situation. She was good at conversation, especially with men.

She knew how to keep the chit-chat going. I tried to emulate that with varying degrees of success.

If it was just me, my mother talked mainly about herself. If there was a man around, she talked about him. She flattered his looks, his taste, his value to the world, his humor, his intelligence—and his generosity. That very few of the men she dated had any of these qualities in abundance never seemed to matter. They all believed her.

I was warming up to say something about what a good doctor Edward was, when he said, "I really admire you. Most guys your age would not be caught dead in a small Michigan town taking care of their grandmother."

"Oh, well..." I fumbled.

He smiled at me. "You need to learn to take compliments. I suspect you're going to have a life full of them."

Wow, he'd missed the boat on that one. I was great at taking compliments, about my pretty eyes and my perky little ass and my snarky quips... I'd just never gotten one for taking care of my grandmother.

Really? That was worth a compliment?

"You should tell me more about yourself," I suggested.

So, Edward told me some things about his growing up in a small town on the other side of Michigan. Honestly, it wasn't that interesting. What I really wanted to know was what it was like to be as pretty as he was. Being good-looking has gotten me lots of things I wanted. Edward was devastatingly handsome. People must trip over themselves giving him things.

Oh crap, he asked me a question and I completely didn't hear it. I'd been lost in the perfect symmetry of his face, the dark blue his eyes had turned in the dim light of the restaurant, the squareness of his chin, his glowing skin, a pulsing vein in his neck which made me wish I was a vampire.

"I'm sorry, what did you say?"

"I asked about your childhood."

"Boring really."

But was it? I remembered a dozen apartments—one of which my mother owned, at least for a while; seven different neighborhoods; and five grammar schools. I did well in school. It was a sort of revenge on my mother who hated school and encouraged me to hate it as well.

"You could be a little more specific," he suggested.

Then I realized I couldn't tell him the truth. That I'd been dragged through my mother's many failed relationships, that we'd moved suddenly and often, that I'd been bullied in good schools and bad. No, that wasn't going to work. One thing I'd learned over drinks in West Hollywood was that guys didn't want to hear about your tough childhood. It frightened them, even if it wasn't your fault.

"Well, my mother was a single mom. She worked really hard to keep a roof over our head."

Kind of true.

"She always put me first."

Not true at all.

He gave me a dubious smile. He wasn't buying this. And that meant I probably wouldn't be living happily ever after with the most beautiful doctor in the world. Ah, well.

"Where is your mother?"

"California."

"She didn't come out when your grandmother had her stroke?"

"Um, well, she's married now."

Lie!

"Her husband's health isn't good. She needed to stay with him."

Super lie!

"What's wrong with him?"

Oh God, a doctor would ask that. Quickly, I calculated the likelihood of Edward's ever meeting my mother or her boyfriends and decided, "He has lung cancer. Stage six."

"Stage six. That *is* serious."

"I know."

Our salads arrived. Caesar, the only salad they served. But that was fine. It was wonderful. The conversation got easier. I asked Edward to tell me funny stories about the ER. He tried to but didn't do such a great job. He didn't seem to want to criticize anyone which, to me, seemed the core of any funny story.

"So have you ever had a patient come in with a lightbulb up their butt?" I asked.

"No. I think that's an urban myth."

"This is a rural area. Maybe it happens in bigger cities."

"Maybe. I'm just as glad I've never had to deal with that kind of extraction."

My steak was fabulous, and there were long pauses while I chewed. In between I attempted to turn the conversation to things I understood well, like *Sex and the City* and *America's Next Top Model*.

"Do you think *Sex and the City* is ending because the girls hate each other?" I asked, though Edward seemed a little confused by the question.

"I don't get a lot of backstage gossip in the ER."

"You probably would if you lived in L.A." Which, to me, was the perfect reason to leave Wyandot County for L.A.

He attempted to talk politics, but it went right over my head. Apparently, there were protests in Tehran—probably because they didn't get *Sex in the City* there. Seriously, if they just gave HBO to everyone in the world peace would breakout everywhere.

I couldn't believe how well it was going. Who would've ever thought I'd come to Masons Bay and find a man like this? He thought taking care of Nana Cole was, like, admirable. Seriously? Well, maybe it was. And then maybe Edward was my gift for taking care of her.

Well, not directly. I didn't think there was some kind of Santa Claus in the sky checking off boxes, like: Took care of old lady; give him a hot doctor. Not intellectually, at least. Emotionally though, emotionally I could totally believe it. He *was* my gift for being good—even if I hadn't exactly been good on purpose.

As much as I wanted dessert, I turned it down. My plan was to have sex with him on the first date, and I didn't want too much in my stomach. The wine and the steak and the salad and the popcorn perch were more than enough. He got the bill and paid it. I didn't even offer to go dutch; I never did.

"Next time it's on you," he said with a charming smile.

"How do you feel about Burger King?"

He laughed, a rumbling dark sound.

Once we were out of the restaurant, he said, "Do you want to go for a little walk?"

"No, we can just go to your place."

Edward laughed again. Apparently, I missed my calling as a comedian. He said, "I appreciate your enthusiasm, but I think I'd like to wait."

"Oh, you don't like me."

"I like you a lot. That's why I want to wait."

"Well, that doesn't make any sense."

"Casual doesn't work out for me."

And that made me ask myself, 'Did it work out for me?' When I lived in L.A. it happened a lot, and sometimes it was fun. Was that what it meant to 'work out'? That it was fun? Or did he mean 'work out' as in something longer. Deeper.

And then, in front of my grandmother's Escalade, he kissed me. Deeply. Passionately. Right there on the sidewalk. It was every bit as good as the meth-fueled kiss I'd had with Denny. But I was confident that the rest of the sex would be just as electric.

He stopped the kiss and left me standing there.

Gasping.

CHAPTER SEVENTEEN

Sunday was a bore. Well, worse than a bore. When I woke up, I realized it was gay pride in Los Angeles. Instead of spending the day getting sunburned and drunk with few hundred thousand of my closest friends, I was in The Middle of Nowhere, Michigan, taking care of a grumpy, homophobic old lady. I spent the afternoon drifting through dreams of dreamy doctors whisking me away to a better future.

Monday morning, I got up early and let my dog out, made Nana Cole's breakfast, then went to help her out of bed. That earned me a good shove.

"I can do it," she spat.

I reminded her that she had a doctor's appointment that morning. I was hoping I'd be able to leave her alone soon. Honestly, I was getting sick and tired of taking care of her. She was not the world's easiest patient.

Eventually, I got her seated in the kitchen in front of a bowl of oatmeal and a banana. I had a vague memory of a dietician coming into Nana's room at the hospital and explaining she shouldn't have eggs or bacon or sausages. Or maybe nobody explained that. Maybe we just got a pamphlet. Either way, it didn't leave a whole lot of choices for breakfast.

"I hate oatmeal."

"I think we've covered that."

Luckily, my cell phone rang so I didn't have to listen to her complain. I didn't recognize the number, but it was local so I figured it was safe to pick up. Or at least safe-ish. It was Hanging Chad.

"I have some information. When do you think you can come into the library? Later today?"

"I don't think so. I'm not sure. What did you find out?"

Obviously, he wanted to do this in person, but I really wanted the information. After a moment, he cleared his throat and began: "So, my friend found some articles that might be relevant. The database they're using just tells you that your search terms are present in particular articles. My friend, who works at the library in Evanston—did I tell you that all ready?"

"Uh, yeah."

"Oh, okay. Anyway, she *was* able to print the articles out. She faxed them last night."

"Okay. What do they say?"

"Well, R. Hessel was arrested—"

"Wait, who's R. Hessel?"

"Richard Christopher Hessel. As soon as I figured that out, we did another search and got an article with the following headline: *Church Leader Arrested for Meth Possession.*"

"Shit," I said.

"You watch your mouth, young man," my grandmother said, obviously preferring to eavesdrop rather than eat her oatmeal. I called Reilly and walked outside. As I watched my dog bound off toward the raised gardens (unplanted this year), I asked Hanging Chad, "Is that article as bad as it sounds?"

"He got stopped for driving erratically. They impounded his car, which meant they had to inventory it—did you know they could do that? It's sort of a work-around for not having a warrant. Anyway, they found four grams of methamphetamine in a gym bag."

"Shit," I said again, this time no one scolded me. "When was this?"

"1999."

"What else did you find?"

"He went to prison for three years."

"He would have gotten out last year."

"It's unlikely he served the whole time. He was probably on parole until last year."

"Is that all you found?"

"There were some other things that weren't really important. He's mentioned in the West Milton First Church of Christ's Christmas Service as the choir leader. There are a couple of other mentions like that."

"Thanks," I said. "I appreciate it."

"Did you want me to save these faxes? You can stop in and pick them up?"

"Sure, I'll do that."

I hung up. This was bad. This was very bad. My grandmother had a stroke when I came out to her. How was she going to react when I told her that her beloved minister was a meth addict? And then my mind clicked over to another possibility. What if he...

I mean, it wasn't *im*possible. A lot of guys up here did it. What if he was like Denny? What if Reverend Hessel was into PNP?

Maybe I just had a dirty mind. But... it wasn't that far-fetched. The AOL chat rooms were filled with married guys who wanted you to be discreet. It wasn't that big a stretch to think that Reverend Hessel might be one of them.

Wait, had he held my hand just a bit too long at the hospital? Had he subtly... Ick!

I might be wrong. I certainly knew guys who thought everyone was gay, so maybe it wasn't true at all. I was probably being an idiot.

But if it were true, it would literally kill my Nana Cole.

The first time she had a stroke was not my fault. I had no idea that might happen if I came out to her. But now? Now I knew. I couldn't tell her that her minister was using meth and sleeping with guys (if that did turn out to be true) because I knew what could happen. I'd need sedatives and a cardiac team on hand if I told her.

But I wouldn't. Couldn't. And there went the money. Crap. I was going to have to shut this whole thing down before she paid me. Seriously, though, this couldn't go any further. I was not going to kill my grandmother in hopes of getting two thousand dollars, no matter how much I needed it.

I stood in back of the house looking at the blue, cloudless sky. For some reason I'd never considered that the sky seemed bigger here. It probably had to do with the fact there weren't a lot of buildings nearby. The only ones I could see were Jasper's house—a white two-story, clapboard with a startling red metal roof—and his bruised and weathered barn. Other than that, there was nothing but gentle hills and fields and trees for a very long way.

I couldn't tell you why I was thinking about the sky. Mostly, I had a sinking feeling in my stomach that I'd be spending the rest of my life in Masons Bay, which was about as appealing as being buried alive in a pine box.

I called for Reilly, but he didn't come. He'd probably found something disgusting to roll in. It was fine. Nana Cole's doctor's appointment was about a half an hour away. By the time we got back from the doctor, Reilly would be ready to come inside.

After I got my grandmother situated in the SUV and before we'd reached the M22 at the end of the drive, she said, "Maybe we should go talk to Ivy Greene again. You know, if someone's going to kill you it's probably someone who cares about you. I think that was on the *Today Show*. Matt Lauer was talking about it, I think."

She was right, of course. It might be Ivy Greene. She

wouldn't be the first person to slip out of a bar to commit a crime and hope no one noticed she was gone. The thing was, if she did kill her husband, she did it because he was a tweaker. Or worse. And I didn't want Nana Cole to find that out.

"We need to stop," I said, as simply as possible. "We should focus on your getting better."

"What?" she asked, clearly confused.

"I don't think we should ask any more questions about Reverend Hessel."

"Well then I'm not going to give you the money."

"I know. That's fine."

I kept my eyes glued to the road. I could feel her glaring at me. Probably not believing a word I said.

"I am better. Even if we're not focused on it. I'm probably getting better *because* we're not focused on it."

"Well, good. I want you to get better."

"So you can go back to Los Angeles?"

"That's the plan."

"Is it really so terrible here?"

Was it? Terrible? I did just have a date with a very hot doctor. And I wasn't paying rent. And I had an excellent doctor giving me more Oxy than I could use. And I didn't end each day smelling like a coffee bean. I mean, maybe it wasn't *that* awful.

On the other hand, the weather sucked. And there was nothing even remotely resembling Santa Monica Boulevard. Even the singular gay bar wasn't all that gay. And you never saw a movie star. And there was no sense that something amazing was right around the corner.

"I asked you a question," Nana Cole said. "Is it really so terrible here?"

Shrugging, I said, "It is what it is," as I pulled up in front of the doctor's office. Dr. Blinski's office was in the front half of an ancient house built of river rock. I think he lived in the back half house.

I guided my grandmother out of the SUV, up three steps to the house, and into the waiting room. There was a window for Dr. Blinski's nurse—a sour-looking woman in her forties. She looked up when we walked in, and said, "Good morning, Mrs. Cole."

"How are you, Nancy?"

"Well, I've been better. What about you?"

"I'm doing well, thank you. What's wrong?"

"My daughter's getting married," she said glumly.

"You don't like her young man?"

"Actually, he's a wonderful boy. But he's Black. I'm just afraid of what their lives will be like."

My first thought was how did she find a Black boy up here? Meanwhile, my grandmother said, "Mmmhmph," probably in an attempt to swallow an opinion or two.

To be helpful, I said, "Things aren't as bad as they used to be."

"Don't pay any attention to him. He's from L.A."

"You're from L.A. and you think things are better? They beat Black men in the street out there."

Crap. She was talking about Rodney King. When was that? I was a teenager. Fourteen? Fifteen? All I could think to say was, "Not recently," followed by, "Excuse me."

I sat down in one of the chairs, which made my grandmother turn around and give me a frosty look. "What are you doing?"

"Waiting. It's a waiting room."

"You can go."

"What do you mean, I can go?"

"You don't need to come in with me anymore. I'm just fine." I'd been attending her doctor's appointments for the last two months. At first there was a question about whether she understood and then, well, it had become habit.

"You can find something more useful to do," she said.

I wondered what exactly she thought I'd do. But then I stood up and said, "Fine. I'll be back in forty-five minutes."

"Make it an hour," Nancy said. "Dr. Blinski is running a bit behind.

Outside, sitting in the Escalade, I wondered exactly what useful thing I could do. The only useful things I'd been doing were taking care of my grandmother and investigating Reverend Hessel's murder. Apparently, I didn't need to do either of those things anymore. So what exactly should I do?

Fifteen minutes later, I was standing in the doorway to Detective Lehmann's office. It took a bit, but I finally decided if I wasn't going to investigate Reverend Hessel's murder any longer I should probably share what I knew with Detective Lehmann.

"I'm done. I don't want to know anything else about Reverend Hessel's murder."

"So, what are you doing here?"

"I came to tell you what I found out."

"Okay. Shoot."

"Reverend Richard Christopher Hessel has a record."

"Richard Hessel? A record?" he asked, faking confusion. "Yes, I knew about Hessel's record. I knew the day after he died. We have his fingerprints."

"Oh, yeah. So did the church know?"

"I don't think so. I doubt they did much in the way of vetting. And... he never gave them much information."

I thought about all the paperwork I had to fill out just to sell coffee drinks, so I asked, "But they were paying him, weren't they?"

"He was paid through an LLC."

"What's that?"

"It's a simple kind of corporation. They paid his company then he paid himself."

"Did he make a lot of money?"

"No. It's not a normal kind of thing. He claimed to do

music gigs on the side, but no one remembers him doing any. Mostly, I think he lived off Ivy Greene."

I think he realized he was a being a bit too chatty because he stopped and asked, "Do you have any other revelations?"

"So, it might not have been an addict caught in the midst of a robbery. It might have been a drug deal gone wrong."

He smiled at me.

"And that's what you've thought since the start, isn't it?"

"I don't want to hear you've been nosing around the local drug dealers, okay?"

"Yeah, okay. I mean, I just said I was done, right?" I hesitated a moment, then said, "Hessel blackmailed Sue Langtree and Reverend Wilkie out of their positions."

"They were boning, huh? I kinda thought that."

"No, they weren't, but it doesn't matter."

"What do you mean it doesn't matter? I thought you came here to tell me what you know."

"Yeah, but this could hurt someone if it came out." I don't know why exactly, but there was something about Bekah Springer that made me not want to see her get hurt.

"Murder is like that. People get hurt."

I decided to give him part of the truth. "They helped a particular person get an abortion. That's what Hessel blackmailed them with."

"So they still have a motive."

"They do, but... then what about the drug connection?"

"Let's stick to what you found out and not what you think, okay?"

"Ivy Greene is the one who called 911."

"I know that."

"Why? Why was she the one to call?"

"She sent her son over to check on Hessel. When he found the body, he called his mother. She called 911 from their house."

That seemed like a fairly reasonable explanation, but it

still bothered me. I wondered if he'd checked all the phone records. Or had they told him? But then I reminded myself I was done with this. I didn't need to know.

"Reverend Hessel claimed to have family in the area but then later denied it. Do you know if he has family nearby?"

"The only family I've found is in Wisconsin. They're estranged and haven't spoken to him since the mid-nineties. He was probably lying. Shocking, I know."

"But why?"

He shrugged, and said, "I don't think it has much to do with his being murdered. So, it's not important." Before I could ask anything else, he said, "I thought you said you're done with this."

"I am."

"Then why are you still standing here?"

CHAPTER EIGHTEEN

None of it really mattered. It didn't matter that we'd probably never find out who killed Reverend Hessel (I hadn't much confidence in Detective Lehmann). And it didn't matter that I didn't have enough money to get home. The important thing was... I was dating a doctor. Or rather, I WAS DATING A DOCTOR!

Yes, there was a part of me, a big part, that wished I could say I was dating a doctor as in Beverly-Hills-plastic-surgeon, but I couldn't. I had to deal with reality. *And*, just because I was dating a small-town trauma doctor didn't mean he wouldn't be willing to move across the country and change his specialty. C'mon, stranger things have happened.

Anyway, when I returned to Dr. Blinski's office, Nana Cole was standing on the sidewalk. She no longer had a walker. Instead, she was sporting a very sturdy looking metal cane with four prongs at the bottom for balance. As soon as she saw me, she wobbled across the grass to the curb.

I jumped out of the SUV and ran around to help her in. After I opened the passenger door, I attempted to help guide her, but she slapped my hands away. I stood back, crossed my arms across my chest, and watched as she ungracefully wrenched her way into the vehicle.

Shaking my head, I walked around the SUV and got in. As I pulled away from the curb, I asked, "Is it safe to leave you alone?"

"Yes, Dr. Blinski said it was safe to leave me alone. Not more than eight hours. You can go back to work now."

That part was not exciting. I didn't have much interest in tromping around people's back forty. Yeah, I know, I had to do something with my life. And since I wasn't exactly sure what that thing was, I might as well do this. Except, I already knew I didn't want to work for the Conservancy forever. Or even another month.

When we reached the end of the driveway I turned off the Escalade, and said, "Wait until I get around to that side before you—"

"Let's just sit for a minute."

"Huh?"

It was awfully quiet. Even for Masons Bay. Finally, she said, "Do you know how many generations of our family have lived on this farm?"

"Not a clue," I said, truthfully.

"Your mother never talked about it?"

The only thing she ever said about the farm was how much she hated it.

"Well, we've been here six generations."

"You mean, my family. It was Grampa Cole's farm."

"No, it came to me. My grandfather was the first Scheck. I think his family was here for a while. He came from back East at the end of the Great Land Rush. Around the time the county was founded. There was a lot of land then."

There was still a lot of land, but okay.

"We grew corn before the Civil War, but then planted orchards around the turn of the century. She meant the last century, not the recent one.

"Does this story have a point?" I asked.

"You don't feel any connection?"

"No."

For a moment, she looked like she'd just taken a punch. Then, ignoring my request, she opened the passenger door.

"Wait," I snapped, jumping out. I ran around the Escalade to find her clutching the door with her cane on the ground. I picked up the cane, set it where she could reach it and then peeled her off the door.

Watching her every step, I walked her over to the back door. As we went, I said, "You really need to learn patience."

"Like you can talk."

That was at least a little bit true, so I didn't say anything. Reaching the back door, I could see there was yet another casserole sitting on the stoop. *My God, did these people do nothing else?*

"Who's it from?" Nana Cole asked me.

Naturally, I had no clue. "Don't you recognize the baking dish?"

"Well, yes, it's brand new and it came from Meijer."

"There's no note," I said, even though I'd taken in a couple of casseroles that hadn't had them. Most of them were given by hand with a few words of sympathy and encouragement. Not to mention instructions for heating.

"It looks like lasagna," she said, as I put it on the counter. "Spinach."

"We can have it for dinner," I said, though I planned to pass. I found spinach disgusting.

"All right."

"Do you want me to make you a sandwich?"

"I'll make my own lunch. You should go out and have some fun."

Where did she think we were? Fun? In Masons Bay? Those thoughts must have flashed across my face because she said, "Call your friend with the colorful hair."

"Friend is stretching it. And I don't think she knows how to have fun."

"Weren't you with her on Saturday night?"

I'd managed to slip out of the house without letting her or Bev know I was going on a date. I hardly wanted to talk about it now, though.

"Fine. I'll go."

I ran upstairs, took an Oxy, and changed into a lavender dress shirt that I liked with a pair of dark jeans. It was a Monday afternoon, after all. I couldn't wear anything actually cool.

A half an hour later, I was in Bellflower. It was not exactly large, but larger than Masons Bay. I popped into the bookstore, Vertical Books, and picked up *GQ, People* and *Vogue*. Then I walked down to Drip.

I got myself a latte with normal milk and two gooey brownies—you know, lunch. Then I settled myself at a tiny café table for two and began to study the magazines I'd bought.

People was asking the nearly impossible question, who was the hottest bachelor, Prince William or Ashton Kutcher? Honestly, I couldn't be sure until I'd slept with them both... though obviously I was leaning toward Prince William since he came with an eventual crown.

On the other hand, the new Hulk was on the cover of *GQ* and, in opinion, they should really throw him into the mix. Demi Moore was on the cover of *Vogue*, which I got for the ads much more than the articles.

My latte and both of the brownies were nearly gone when Carl walked into the coffeeshop. I nearly didn't look up from *GQ*'s guide to fall clothes. Too much brown in my opinion. There was always too much brown in the fall.

Carl got a coffee and found a table against the far wall. I picked up my magazines and went up to the counter to order another latte. I waited for it, thinking about Carl. I was not trying to find out who'd killed his stepfather. That was over. But he was still a bisexual male.

Not that I wanted to sleep with him, he was just someone I could flirt with. And clearly after my date on Saturday I was out of practice. The fact that he or his mother still might be a murderer was hardly a deterrent.

"Hey," I said, sliding my refilled latte onto the table. Quickly, it was followed by my magazines. "Fancy meeting you here."

"Um, I come here a lot."

"Well, there's nowhere else, really. Is there?" I fake laughed.

"So why did you think it was weird that I'm here?"

"I didn't think—it's just an expression."

He didn't say anything. I took a sip of my latte. I was beginning to feel the caffeine from the first one. Even after an Oxy.

"Do you like magazines?"

"Not really?"

"Books?"

He shook his head.

"Music?"

"No."

"So you're just going to sit here and drink coffee."

"It's a coffeehouse."

This was going nowhere. I almost got up to pick out another table, but then I thought, *Oh, what the hell.*

"Did you know your stepfather was using meth?" I asked, very casually.

He abruptly stood up. I thought he was going to walk away, but then Opal was there standing behind me. I turned and saw that she was wearing a black leotard and a giant vintage scarf. Her hair was fading. She wasn't taking care of it.

"What are you doing here?" she snapped at me. "You need to leave people alone."

She kissed Carl's cheek. He tolerated it.

"My grandmother told me to go out and have some fun," I said, quite truthfully.

"Fun?" Carl said. "You just told me my stepfather was using meth. Is that your idea of fun?"

"What? That's not true," Opal said, sitting down.

"It is true," I said. "He was arrested for possession in Chicago. The police know all about it. They think he was murdered in a drug deal gone wrong."

"Did you know?" Opal asked Carl.

"No. No, I didn't," he said, not looking up. He was totally lying.

Ignoring me, Opal said, "But your stepfather's behavior... It must have been suspicious."

"He wasn't always around. He saw a lot of his parishioners at the church office. And, you know, he had insomnia a lot. Then he'd be kind of angry and depressed because he didn't get enough sleep."

"Where would he have gotten the money?" I asked. Yes, I'm obsessed with money. Get over yourself.

"My mother gave him whatever he wanted."

"Did that make you mad?"

"Why would it—no, that's just who she is." After the briefest pause, he added, "She wasn't happy. That made me mad."

"Do you think she might have known? About the meth, I mean."

"I don't think so. I don't think she'd have put up with it."

"Do you think she could have killed him?"

"Henry!" Opal said. "Ivy couldn't do that!"

But Carl was not as quick. "No... no I don't think she could have killed him. If she'd known I think she would have turned him in to the police. I think that's how she'd have dealt with it."

"Did she ever catch you with drugs? When you were a teenager?"

"Once. Yeah."

"And she turned you in to the police?"

"No. I was fourteen, though. And it was just pot."

I wondered what he was doing. It felt like he was throwing his own mother under a bus. I mean, he said she wouldn't have killed Hessel, but it didn't feel like he meant it. So, had she killed him? Or did he just want me to think she had?

"What do you guys do for fun around here?" I asked.

They looked at me like I just asked where they hid the human-skin wearing cannibals. Honestly, I'd wondered about that for a long time. Fun, I mean.

"What? It's a pretty normal question."

"We go tubing," Carl offered. "That's fun."

"On the Beckett River."

I flinched a little. The guy who'd tried to kill me was a Beckett. And so was the guy he'd killed. For that matter, so was I. Which didn't mean I enjoyed hearing about more Becketts. Even geographical ones.

"It's almost twenty miles long. You stick your butt into a giant tire tube, drop a six pack into the water, and float away. By the time you reach the end the six pack is gone."

"How do you get back?"

"We leave cars at both ends."

"You get a lot of DUIs?"

"Not yet.

"Or should I say: Tubing While Intoxicated."

"Ha-ha."

"When's the next time you're going?" I asked. I was not trying to invite myself along. Really. It was just the polite thing to ask.

"I probably won't go this summer," Opal said. "I got pretty scalded last year."

"You need a coffee," Carl said. "Let me get it."

He didn't ask for her order, so he must have known her

regular. The moment he was gone, I asked her, "So, you weren't clear before. Did you fuck him?"

"It's not like that."

I waited.

"We tried to do it once when we were seventeen, but it was a nonstarter."

"You said he's bi?" I asked, dubiously. I mean, her story didn't strike me as very bi. Sure, she wasn't Jennifer Aniston, but teenage boys were hardly picky. Believe me, I know. When I was thirteen, I had a deep and meaningful relationship with a standard-sized pillow. And no, I am not a pillow-sexual.

"Yes, he's bi," she whispered. "And keep your voice down. You don't need to tell everyone in Wyandot County."

I decided it was probably best to let her think what she wanted to think. And who knows, maybe she was right. My gaydar was set to Kinsey-6. Bi guys, curious guys—they just confused me.

"You guys have been friends since then?"

"Yes, we're very close."

"That's nice. It's good to have friends."

She looked at me like I'd just sprouted antlers.

CHAPTER NINETEEN

Somewhere along the line it had begun raining. Heavy gray clouds turned the sky dark, even though it wasn't even five in the afternoon and it would be light until nearly ten. Something about being so far north or time zones or both, I don't know. But the last few days had been insanely bright.

When I opened the back door, Reilly was whimpering. "Do you have to go outie?" I asked the dog. Yes, I spoke baby talk to my dog, as though I thought by doing so he'd eventually pick up the language. He hadn't and he wouldn't.

I opened the back door for him, but he didn't budge.

"Okay." I turned my back and he whimpered again. Except it wasn't him. He wasn't the one whimpering. My first thought was 'Oh God!'

Then I called out, "Nana?"

The hair on the back of my neck stood up as I walked down the short hallway to the bathroom. It was between the kitchen and my grandmother's bedroom.

"Nana, are you okay?"

I knocked on the bathroom door and then pushed it open. There she was lying on the floor in a fetal position. There was foamy vomit on the floor and on her chin. Obviously, she'd had another stroke.

My stomach clenched. Oh my God, she was going to die! And that was terrible! I'd just started to almost, maybe, like her! Of course, looking on the bright side, it was not my fault this time.

"Nana can you hear me?"

"Will? Will is that you? I'm sorry. I was bad. I shouldn't have—I lost the baby, Will. Can you forgive me? Can you ever forgive me?"

I bent over and she clutched at me as though she'd never let me go. Clearly, she had no idea who I was.

"Nana? It's me, Henry. Your grandson. I'm going to call an ambulance."

"Where is Will? I want Will. Why won't he come? Did you make him go away?"

"Don't try to get up. Just stay there."

The smell was terrible. She hadn't only thrown up on the floor, she'd also vomited into the toilet. I flushed it. Back in the kitchen, I used the wall phone to call 911.

As I gave the operator our address, I could hear my grandmother vomiting again. This was different from her first stroke. That time she hadn't vomited at all. Maybe this was affecting a different part of her brain? Maybe that meant it wouldn't be as bad. Maybe it meant she *wouldn't* die.

I was told the ambulance would be there in about ten minutes. I was also told to stay on the line, but I said I needed to go back into the bathroom to be with my grandmother. I didn't want to leave her alone. Then I hung up.

Back in the bathroom, I said, "The ambulance is coming, Nana."

"What ambulance, Will? You can take me to the hospital. I'm not hurt bad. Honest. I don't want you making a fuss. I love you. I love you so much."

This was embarrassing.

"It's Henry, Nana. Your grandson."

"What?"

"I'm Henry."

"Yes, I know that. You look just like your grandfather."

It felt like she meant Will, the man she'd mistaken me for, so I said, "My grandfather was Samuel."

"Why are you telling me that? I know who your grandfather was."

"Okay, that's good."

This couldn't be as serious as the first stroke since she could still talk to me clearly. Right?

"How's your head? Do you have a headache?"

"No. Why would I have a headache?"

"Because you're having another stroke. Remember, you had a bad headache the first time you had a stroke."

I could tell I was confusing her. It was like suddenly she couldn't remember that she'd had a stroke. I could hear the siren as the ambulance turned down our long driveway. They'd arrived quickly.

"I'm going to let them in."

As I opened the door to the paramedics, I blurted out that my grandmother was having another stroke.

"Another?"

That left me explaining her recent medical history, even as I led them to the bathroom. Quickly, they put in an IV. They asked her a few questions, and then one of them said, "She seems pretty cognoscente."

"Yeah, a few minutes ago she thought I was her first husband."

"I did *not*," she said, clearly offended. "I don't know what you're talking about."

Then she puked again, moaning even as she retched. One of the paramedics said, "We'll be transporting her in a few minutes. Do you want to ride with her in the ambulance?"

"No, I'll bring the car." That way I had a way to get home.

I also wouldn't have to watch her throw up, which was making my stomach turn.

I followed the ambulance along the rain-slicked roads to the hospital in Bellflower. Part of me worried that I was losing her, while another part wondered what that would mean. My mother would get the farm, of course, and she'd immediately sell it, also of course. If I asked nicely enough—and by nicely, I mean begged—she might give me some money to help get me back on my feet and set up back home in Los Angeles.

Thinking that made me feel bad. My grandmother wasn't dead. Yet. So I shouldn't be thinking about how well that might work out for me. Though it did seem like it could work out very well... I mean, it would be better if she just left me some money directly, but that certainly wouldn't happen.

And then, randomly, I started thinking about how much she'd hate the farm being sold. Was that why she'd talked about her family and how many—oh my God. She wanted me to talk my mother out of selling it when she died. Hmmm. That was not a conversation I had any interest in. Nor one I expected would be successful. My mother had always done exactly as she damn well pleased. No matter how it affected me.

Anyway, Midland Hospital (formerly Morley Medical Center, formerly St. Anne's) was not especially busy, so it wasn't that hard to find a parking spot near the emergency room and hurry over to join my grandmother before she got all the way inside.

I suppose I should have wondered if Edward was working, but I hadn't, so it was a surprise when he walked into the examining area they'd settled us in. I immediately turned into a five-foot-eight stick of melting butter.

"Hi," I gurgled foolishly. "I think my grandmother has had another stroke."

"I have not," she said from the narrow bed beside me.

"It's probably a mild one," I said, explaining the fact that she was speaking coherently. "She was vomiting and disoriented."

"Hello, Emma, do you remember me?"

"No."

"I'm Dr. Stewart. We met about two months ago when you had your stroke."

"Oh. Okay." She looked flustered. I suspected she was having the same reaction to his good looks that I had. The tree doesn't fall very far from the apple, as it were.

"Do you remember what happened?"

"I heated up some lasagna for my lunch. A while later I began to feel sick."

"What's a while?"

"I don't know. It might have only been a half an hour."

"Did the lasagna have sausage in it?"

"No. It was spinach."

I was tempted to add "Bluch."

"We'll need to run some tests. I don't think you've had another stroke, though."

"She hasn't? Well, what's wrong with her?"

"I'm not sure. That's what the tests are for. How do you feel now, Emma?"

"Queasy."

"I'll have the nurse bring you something to settle your stomach."

And with that, he was gone. The light seemed to have left the curtained room. I said to my grandmother, "I thought you wanted the lasagna for dinner?"

"I changed my mind."

"Did it taste all right? It didn't taste like it had turned, did it?" I asked. Given Edward's questions it was obvious he was leaning toward food poisoning.

"It tasted fine. Maybe a little bitter. I don't know. I was hungry."

I suppose it didn't matter when she ate the lasagna. Given that I can't stand spinach I wouldn't have touched it.

"He's a very attractive young man."

"Mmmm-hmmm."

"I wonder if he's single?"

"He's too young for you," I told her.

"Not for me. For a young girl who goes to our church."

"A young girl?"

"Well, young to me. I think she's almost forty."

"Dr. Stewart is only thirty-one."

"How do you know how old he is?"

"He looks thirty-one."

"I wonder if he'd go out with her?"

"I doubt it." This was an uncomfortable topic, so I attempted to move her off it. "You should focus on getting better. You can pimp out your fellow congregants later on."

"I'm not a pimp—that's a disgusting thing to say."

"Well, what do you think is going to happen? You set them up on a date, then what?"

"If they like each other they'll go on another date."

"And if they keep liking each other they'll end up doing *it*." Of course, I knew this wouldn't happen with Edward. I was just pretending it might to annoy my grandmother.

"They could get married," she said.

"And that would make you a really, really good pimp."

"Oh shush," she said. "I don't know what you're talking about."

That's when the nurse came in. She was an attractive young woman of about twenty-five. Exactly the kind of girl my grandmother would enjoy pimping out—to me.

First, she gave Nana Cole a quick shot of something to help with the nausea. Then, she poked at my grandmother's arm—the one that didn't have an IV in it—until she found a vein and took a few vials of blood. Then she scurried out of the room.

"She was pretty," Nana Cole said.

"Maybe she'd like to go out with Ed—Dr. Stewart."

She squinted her eyes at me, and then asked, "Did you have fun?"

"Watching the nurse draw your blood?"

"No. I sent you out to have some fun. Did you have any?"

"I guess."

"What did you do?"

"I went to Drip. It's a coffee—"

"I know what it is. Did you see anyone?"

"I ran into that girl Opal. And Carl, Ivy's son."

"They're a sweet couple."

"They're not—" I started and then decided it might be better to let her think whatever she wanted to think. "Yes, they're a sweet couple."

I waited for her to ask if Opal had any friends for me or if there were any pretty girls at the coffee shop. Remarkably, she did not. She grew quiet and there was a heavy frown on her face. I imagined she was contemplating her mortality. Given the situation it seemed likely. But then she asked, "Do you think Carl killed Reverend Hessel?"

That sort of put a damper on Opal and Carl being a sweet couple thing.

"He has an alibi. He was with Opal. His mother was in a bar. It's possible she slipped—"

"But Ivy had no reason to kill her husband, did she?"

"None that I know of," I bald-faced lied. If she'd learned about his drug-addiction and his possible, probable addiction to PNP—well, if she'd found out, that would be a motive, a big one.

"Just because we don't know doesn't mean she didn't have a motive."

"I'm sure the police will figure it out," I said.

We waited quietly for a bit. A long bit. Eventually, I asked, "Should I call my mother?"

"I'm not dying."

"So that's the bar? I should only call her if you're dying?"

"There's nothing she can do. I'll call her tomorrow, I promise."

That really annoyed me. My mother had completely disengaged from my grandmother's care. Dumping it all on me. It wasn't particularly fair—nor wise. On a good day, I was better than nothing. And that, I'm afraid, is the best you can say about me.

Not that my mother would be an improvement. Mainly I wanted *her* to take care of her mother so I didn't have to.

And then, after what seemed an eternity, Edward walked through the curtains.

"Henry, you didn't eat any of the lasagna, did you?"

"God no. I don't care what Popeye says, spinach is the work of the devil."

He didn't say anything for a moment, so I asked, "You think it's food poisoning?"

"No. I don't."

"Oh."

That was odd. Why did he ask if I'd had some of the lasagna if he didn't think it was food poisoning?

He turned to Nana Cole and smiled. "Well, you're dehydrated, certainly. But the IV should take care of that fairly quickly. Your liver panel is slightly elevated."

"There's something wrong with my liver?"

Edward flipped through my grandmother's file, which obviously included her most recent stay since it was pretty thick. After a moment he said, "I'm not seeing a chronic problem with your liver. I think the elevation may be temporary. I'm afraid you may have been exposed to a toxin."

"So, it is food poisoning," I said.

"No. I don't think so. Emma, what else did you have to eat or drink today?"

"Oatmeal," she said, obviously hoping that was the culprit. "Banana. Tea."

"We should take a look at the lasagna. It could contain some kind of toxin."

I asked, "When you say toxin, you mean..."

"Poison."

CHAPTER TWENTY

Standing in the parking lot outside the ER—cell service inside the hospital sucked—I called Bev. After I explained a little about the situation, I asked her to go to the house and pick up the lasagna. Then I went back into the hospital, to find that Edward had wandered off to take care of his other patients. Looking confused, Nana Cole asked, "Who would want to poison me? People like me."

"It's probably just a misunderstanding," I said, lamely. I knew it wasn't. There's nothing to misunderstand about poison.

"You think it was meant for someone else?"

"You think it was left at the wrong house?" I asked. "That's very unlikely."

"No, I mean... Was it meant for you?"

Oh God, she was still delusional. Well maybe not that delusional. But I'd stopped asking questions about Reverend Hessel. It was over. There was no reason to think anyone had a reason to poison me. Of course, it's not like I'd taken out an ad in the *Eagle*. People didn't necessarily *know* I'd stopped asking questions.

"You have been asking a lot of questions about Reverend Hessel," she noted.

"You asked me to!"

"Well, I didn't think someone would try to kill you."

I suppose she had a point. I might have gotten too close to Reverend Hessel's killer. And whoever that was didn't know I'd stopped asking questions, so they decided to, you know, get rid of me. Or at the very least slow me down. They just hadn't considered the fact that I really couldn't stand spinach.

Sitting in a plastic chair next to my grandmother's bed, I tried to work out who might have baked the deadly casserole—but I didn't get very far since Bev walked in holding the lasagna. A moment later, Edward was back.

"I took a fork and peeked at it. It's not spinach," Bev said.

"Really?" I said. "What is it?"

"I think it might be Solomon's seal or, possibly, baneberry leaves. Of course, it's the berries that are most poisonous. They may have been mixed into the sauce."

"Those are native plants, aren't they?" Edward asked.

Bev nodded.

"Oh my God," I said, thinking, *And people just leave plants like this lying around?*

"Most people up here know that."

"They wouldn't actually kill a person, though" Edward said.

"No," Bev agreed. "But just because people know a plant is poisonous doesn't mean they know the particulars. Most people just know the plants are poisonous and that's it."

And then Detective Lehmann came through the curtain. It was getting quite crowded in that little space. I looked at Edward, who said, "The minute I suspected poisoning I was legally required to call the police."

Detective Lehmann took a look at the lasagna, and asked, "Is that the, uh, delivery device?"

"Yes," Edward said.

"I'll take it then." He opened up a bag he'd brought with him. Bev put the casserole inside.

"I suppose you've all touched the dish?"

"I haven't touched it," Edward said. The rest of us were mute.

"And what do you think is in here?"

"Either Solomon's seal or baneberry leaves," Bev said. "I can't be sure, but it's definitely not spinach. And berries. Possibly berries from either plant. Maybe both."

"Where do you find those?"

"Everywhere. They're native."

Once again, it seemed very foolish to just—

"Oh," Detective Lehmann said, sounding disappointed. "That doesn't exactly narrow things down."

"It wouldn't kill anyone," Bev said. "Well, not an adult. Whoever made the lasagna either didn't know that or just wanted to make Henry sick."

"Bev, we don't know—"

"So, it was left for you, Henry?"

"Probably not. No. It was just left outside on the stoop. There was no note or anything."

"You didn't find that suspicious?"

"People have been dropping off casseroles since my grandmother had her stroke."

"I made a hearty mac 'n' cheese with ham and tomatoes," Bev said.

"Oh, that one was good," I said, and it was. I ate almost all of it myself.

"Do you have any idea who might have done this?" Detective Lehmann asked me.

"Isn't it your job to figure that out?"

"You'd be surprised how often people know exactly who hurt them."

"Well, no, I don't—I mean, I guess it could have been Reverend Hessel's killer. But I don't exactly know who that is."

"Yet," my grandmother added.

I looked at her. Crap, I was going to have to find out who killed the drug addled, possibly, occasionally gay Reverend Hessel. Otherwise, that person might keep trying to kill me. Ugh.

"When can my grandmother leave?" I asked Edward.

"I think it's best if we keep her overnight. It's concerning when anyone her age gets this sick."

"I'm not *that* old."

"I didn't say you were old. We're just concerned when someone your age—"

"That means old."

"The important thing is you're staying the night."

"In that case, I'm going to need the ladies' room," Nana Cole said.

"I'll have a nurse bring you a bed pan," Edward said.

"Oh, no, just have her walk me to the bathroom."

"I'm afraid you need to stay in bed right now."

She gave Edward a look I wouldn't wish on my worst enemy. The rest of us quickly vacated.

I went out to the waiting room and took a seat, thinking about who might have done this. It was someone who knew we wouldn't think twice about accepting a casserole. That only narrowed the field to twenty or so. Well, no, people up here knew bringing a casserole was the right thing to do when someone had an illness or a tragedy. Really, it could have been anyone in the county.

No one in Los Angeles brought you a casserole when you had a tragedy. In fact, if your neighbors knew you'd had a tragedy, they tended to avoid you as though it might be contagious. I still find a certain logic in that.

I went back to checking things off... It had to be someone who knew where we lived. Which didn't narrow the field any further since Nana Cole was listed in the phone book.

And, of course, it had to be the person who killed

Reverend Hessel. *Run through the suspects, one by one*, I told myself. People were often killed by someone close to them. Ivy Greene was in a bar, seen by who knows how many people. Her son, Carl, had been with Opal. So, unless he and Opal did it together it wasn't him.

I considered for a moment whether they might have done it together. Honestly, it seemed ridiculous. It was challenging enough having coffee with Opal, I couldn't imagine she'd stop being annoying long enough to commit murder. But then, Carl did have a better relationship with her than I did... so... maybe.

Or maybe it was Reverend Wilkie and Sue Langtree. Reverend Hessel had blackmailed them both. Of course, they were both ancient, decrepit really. I had trouble believing either of them could bludgeon someone to death.

And what about Denny? Maybe my questions had been a little obvious. Maybe he'd guessed I was trying to find Reverend Hessel's killer. Which might possibly be him—

I looked up and there was Edward standing over me. I nearly swooned. Thankfully, I didn't. I didn't need another medical bill.

"Are you okay?"

"Oh yeah. I didn't have any of the lasagna. I hate spinach—"

"That's not what I meant. This is the second time your grandmother's been in the hospital in what... two months?"

"Three."

"That has to be frightening."

"It is."

And it was. He smiled at me so sweetly I felt dizzy.

"What time do you get off?" I asked, trying not to sound too eager.

"Six tomorrow morning. I'm on nights for the next week. And then I'm going camping in the UP for the fourth of July."

"Who are you going with?"

God, I sounded jealous, which produced a smirk on

Edward's face. It was probably the most attractive smirk I'd ever seen.

"I'm going with my brother and his family."

"Oh."

"Can I call you when I get back?"

It seemed awfully far away, but I agreed.

NANA COLE WAS RELEASED the next morning around ten. She'd spent the night on the second floor, which was nowhere near the ER so I hadn't gotten to see Edward again. I would have liked to pop into a supply closet with him and make like the sex-crazed Dr. Kovac on *ER,* but I didn't get the chance to suggest that. I did get lost on the second floor thinking about it though.

Once my grandmother was settled, I went home and took a couple of Oxys. Well, maybe three. I woke up the next morning, afternoon, um... shortly after lunch actually, and went to retrieve my grandmother. I managed to get her into the SUV and start the twenty-minute drive before she said, "We can't stop trying to find Reverend Hessel's killer. They tried to kill you. They might try again."

"We? I'm the one looking for his killer. I'm the one they tried to poison. I mean, you made a point of that."

"Well, you're not going to let them try again, are you?"

I did want to continue, knew that I had to really. It's just that there were other considerations. Like my grandmother having a stroke if I told her too much.

"You know, if I find Reverend Hessel's killer I'll probably find out things about the reverend you probably don't want to know."

"Why are you saying that? It was a burglary. You just have to find the burglar."

"I don't think it was a burglary."

I kicked myself. I should have told her that Reverend Hessel had been in prison for drug possession while she was still in the hospital. That way, if she did have a stroke, they could have taken care of her right then and there. Driving *away* from the hospital wasn't exactly the time.

"I think you'd better tell me what he was up to."

On the other hand, I was only five minutes from the ER so I decided to risk—

"Reverend Hessel went to prison for drugs."

"And you didn't want to tell me that?"

"No. I didn't."

"You thought I'd have another stroke."

"Uh-huh."

"You've done drugs, though."

"Well, yeah."

"And your mother certainly has."

"Yes."

"So, there you go. I'm fine."

Of course, if I was right and he was into PNP then that was another thing entirely. A thing I wouldn't tell her. And I might be wrong. I probably *was* wrong.

I sighed as I turned into the driveway. I was going to have to do this. Since someone had tried to poison, us or me, whatever, I had to find out who killed Hessel. Just so my Nana Cole and I didn't wake up dead.

Damn.

CHAPTER TWENTY-ONE

Queens Way Mobile Home Park was a tiny trailer park with only one street running around the park in a perfect square. Ronnie Sheck lived in Number 15, a baby blue singlewide with a pop-out attached part-way down.

The wind had begun to blow, sounding vaguely like a runaway train, slapping me in the face like a damp towel when I climbed out of Nana's Escalade. I walked up to Ronnie's metal door and knocked.

After a moment, he opened the door. Ronnie looked ridiculously young (fifteen) for his age (early thirties), with freckles, scraggly hair full of cowlicks and very little in the way of facial hair. It was like he'd reached a certain age and simply stopped.

"I remember you. You bought some pot and a few Oxy. That was a while ago. Where you been?"

"I had a little car accident that night."

"Oh, that was you. Wow. You hurt yourself?"

"A bit. Yeah."

"And they don't want to give you any more pills, do they? I can give you twenty tens for a hundred and twenty-five."

Given that I was getting more than I was using from Dr.

Blinski for about seventy-five bucks, most of which was the visit, that was a definite no go.

"I'm fine."

"You're fine? Who's your doctor? Blinski?"

"Um, yeah."

"That rat bastard is going to put me out of business." Then he cocked his head. "Unless you wanna sell some?"

"No, that's okay."

"I'll give you twenty bucks for ten pills."

Obviously, the markup was steep.

"Really, no."

"So why are you here?"

"Do you know anything about Reverend Hessel using methamphetamine?"

"I might."

"Did he like to play and party?"

He got quiet. Crap, I was going to have to give him pills. That was the only way I'd get information out of him. But I didn't want to. Yeah, I had a couple pills in my pocket for an emergency and still had a bunch at home. But. I mean. There was a principle here. I didn't want to just hand over...

"I've got two tens on me. That's it."

He held out his hand. Reluctantly, I reached into a pocket and put the foil-wrapped pills into his palm.

"So yeah, I've heard the good reverend liked to PNP." He shrugged. "Each to his own, you know?"

"Who'd you hear it from?"

He shook his head and said, "Not for a couple of measly tens. Sorry."

And then he slammed the door in my face. That's it? That's all I got for my pills? I pounded on the door but gave up after a minute or two. What an asshole.

I GOT BACK to Masons Bay around three. My plan was to get Denny to cut my hair. Ridiculous, I know. It had only been a week since my last haircut. I'd probably come out bald, but I really needed to talk to him and it seemed the safest way.

Taking one of the back streets that ran parallel to Main, I drove past Grover. When I got close to the barbershop, I saw Denny across the street with Carl Burke. They were embroiled in an argument, so I didn't make the turn. I kept going, hoping they hadn't noticed me. As soon as I was out of sight, I did a U turn and crept back toward them. When I could just barely see them, I pulled over and parked. At best I could tell they hadn't noticed me.

Denny was yelling at Carl. Slumped over and shrunken, Carl was red-faced, tears flowing. I lowered both of my front windows to see if I could hear anything they were saying. I couldn't hear much other than the occasional snippet.

"...love you..."

"...anything to do with..."

"...you can't..."

"...stay away..."

"...no, no, no..."

Carl reached for Denny, attempting to put his arms around him. Denny pushed him away. He fell to the ground sobbing. Denny continued to yell at him, then pulled him up. Stumbling away, Carl held an arm over his face and rushed over to a gold Honda Civic hatchback. A pretty new one. I was jealous.

Climbing into the car, Carl sped off. Denny watched, then took a few steps toward the barbershop. I jumped out of the Escalade and hurried over.

"Hey. You okay?"

"What are you doing here?"

"I wasn't spying on you. Honest. But I couldn't help seeing that. What's he so upset about?"

He leaned against his car, folded his arms and stared at me. "You didn't answer my question. What are you doing here?"

"I came to ask you a question about Reverend Hessel."

"How about you leave me alone."

"Well, I guess that answers my question."

And it did, kind of. I wanted to know if he ever PNP'd with the good reverend. Not even letting me ask the question made it seem like a definite yes.

I could see that I'd piqued his curiosity. He wanted to know what my question was. Finally, he asked, "All right. What's the question?"

"I heard you liked to PNP with Reverend Hessel." Not exactly what I'd heard but hey it was my question.

"Where did you hear that?"

"Around. Is that why Carl was upset? Because you were doing it with his stepfather?"

"Carl thinks he's in love with me," he said with a shrug. Like it was something that happened to him all the time.

"How long has he thought that?"

"A while."

"Are you in love with him?"

"It doesn't matter if I am," he said cryptically.

"Because you gotta do what you gotta do?"

"Sometimes I'm short. You know, financially. So I hang out with someone like Chris. It wasn't like I wanted to have sex with him. I just did it to get what I needed. It's not a big deal."

"Except for the part where Hessel is dead."

"I didn't have anything to do with that."

"Did Carl?"

"You'd have to ask him."

"When was the last time you were with Hessel?"

"A few days before he died."

"And Carl found out..."

"He did."

Before I could ask how Carl had found out—though my

guess was coitus interruptus—Denny's father came out of the barbershop and called him. Denny looked over at me, and said, "Don't come back here," then ran back into the barbershop.

I walked back to my car thinking that Carl had to have done it. He had a strong motive. Love, or maybe jealousy. I mean, your own stepfather doing the guy you were hung up on. Killing him just made sense. Except for one thing, of course. Carl had an alibi.

Unless Opal was lying for him. Could she be? Was I wrong to believe her?

MASONS BAY HAD a charming shopping area on Main Street. It consisted of two facing rows of hundred-year-old buildings that looked a little too much like a movie set. Pastiche was a boutique on the west side of the street squeezed between the movie theater and a fudge shop.

Like the other businesses on Main Street, the storefront was narrow, with a high ceiling and a rustic appeal: wooden floors, mismatched furnishings, lux mixed with handmade. The kind of vibe stores paid decorators scads for in L.A. but was probably much more catch-as-catch-can here.

The clothes at Pastiche were largely handmade, and not by tiny hands in Indonesia. That was reflected in the prices, which I was sure were huge. You had to be wealthy to care who made your clothes.

Opal stood next to the cash register. Her hair was even more faded. The green and orange and yellow had washed out, making her head look like a bag of pastel mints. The chalky kind you always want to spit out the minute you put them into your mouth.

"You can't just come in here," she said, when she looked up and saw me.

"Maybe I'm a customer."

"It's a lady's boutique."

"I could be buying my grandmother a gift." I looked around. Was there anything in here my grandmother would want?

"Are you buying her a gift?" Opal demanded.

"Maybe."

"Is it her birthday?"

"No. Early Christmas shopping."

"Very early. What are you looking for?"

"A scarf maybe."

She walked over to a line of scarfs and picked one out. "This one would go well with your grandmother's coloring."

It had about fifteen colors in it, so it probably went with anyone's coloring.

"How much is it?" I asked, bracing myself.

"Three ninety-five."

"Four dollars? Really?" Maybe I would get it for my grandmother. Yeah, it was June and Christmas was ridiculously far off. I could give it to her when I—

"Three *hundred* ninety-five."

"That's insane."

"What do you want? You're not here to buy a scarf."

I realized it was time to get serious, so I said, "Your boyfriend Carl is in love with Denny the hairdresser."

"Denny's a barber."

"Whatever. Denny and Reverend Hessel used to PNP together."

"What's PNP?"

"Party and play."

"Is that what it sounds like?"

I nodded.

"You think Reverend Hessel and Denny... that's stupid."

"Denny admitted it. Didn't Carl say anything to you about it?"

"No."

"You're sure?

"I think I'd remember that."

"He could have come to you and told you what he'd done and asked you to give him an alibi."

"You really think I'm the kind of girl who'd lie for a guy?"

"A guy she loved. Sure."

"Get out."

"You can't throw me out. I'm a customer."

"You're not a customer. You're an asshole. Get out."

"A girl who lied for a guy would throw me out."

That stopped her. She glared at me, pursing her lips and grinding her jaw. "Look, this is what happened. I wasn't planning to see Carl that night. But he called around seven-forty-five, said he wanted to come over and hang out. He got to my house around eight. I had a couple of DVDs I'd rented. *Adaptation*, which was weird, and *The Pianist*, which was depressing. Carl seemed nervous or whatever. Upset maybe, but he wouldn't tell me about what."

"And normally he would tell you?"

"He didn't kill his stepfather," she said. "He couldn't have. According to Detective Lehmann, Reverend Hessel was still alive when Carl got to my house. And he was with me the whole time. It's impossible that he killed him."

CHAPTER TWENTY-TWO

All right, so I guess she had a point. If everyone had their times right, then it was true, Carl couldn't have killed his stepfather. Opal could still be lying, but I didn't have any proof of that. She'd been pretty consistent. So that left me with the same question I'd been asking myself all month: Who killed Reverend Hessel?

It was nearly five when I got home. I was starving, which was ridiculous. Dinner at five in the afternoon was a senior citizen move. Still, I stopped at the refrigerator immediately and poked around looking for a casserole. One that had already been sampled and was clearly *not* poisonous.

I put what looked like some kind of pasta and chicken casserole—no green vegetables in sight—into the oven and went in search of Nana Cole. She was not in the living room watching Fox News, so I walked through the room and cracked open the door to her bedroom. She wasn't in there. I made my way back to the hallway and walked down to the bathroom. The door was standing open and she wasn't in there either. She wasn't anywhere in the house.

Opening the back door, I looked out to see if she was

taking a walk, which would really have been more of a hobble. I didn't see her anywhere on the property. She couldn't have gotten far. I called out her name a few times but quickly gave up.

Of course, she refused to carry her mobile phone. Yes, they were very expensive, but that wasn't the problem. She was highly suspicious of radio waves or whatever kind of wave was used to make them wireless, and completely convinced that the government was attempting to control us through those radio waves. This, I'd found out, was also her rationale for not having a microwave.

The one or two times she'd brought this idea up, I'd bit my tongue. I could have said, if the government really wanted to control us they'd use Fox News. But I hadn't. Mainly because I didn't think she'd get it.

I opened up my flip phone and scrolled to Bev's number. I pressed the call button. Bev answered a couple of rings later.

"I've misplaced my grandmother."

"She's fine, she's here with me."

"Where's here?"

"We're at Barbara's." She lowered her voice to a near whisper. "She heard from the Army. They found her grandson's body."

"Oh." I said, an important contribution to the conversation.

"Emma is looking tired. Could you come and get her?"

"Um, yeah, I guess."

Why couldn't Bev bring her home? I wondered as I hung up. She'd brought her there. Grudgingly, I went out to the Escalade and drove down the driveway. I sat there counting cars as they went by. Three, four, six. Annoyingly, traffic had picked up around Memorial Day.

Tourists. Fudgies.

I know it's ridiculous to complain about traffic in Masons

Bay. I grew up in Los Angeles, after all. Except, I did complain. It was taking forever to get out of my grandmother's driveway. In the summer, it seemed like there was a traffic problem in Wyandot County and probably for the same reason there was a traffic problem in L.A. There were more cars than the roads could—

Ah, a break. Between a PT Cruiser and a Wagoneer pulling an Airstream, I zoomed out onto M22 and then had to immediately slow down. The PT Cruiser was going ten miles an hour below the speed limit.

Masons Bay was ten minutes away in the summer and five in the winter. Yes, I know, I was annoyed about a ten-minute drive, but it was *double* what it should be.

Barbara lived on Saint Pete, which ran parallel to Main Street in Masons Bay Village. There were already half a dozen cars sitting in front of her yellow house. Made of clapboard, the house was built on a slight rise so that the front porch was quite a bit above the street. After I parked the Escalade, I walked down the sidewalk and then climbed the steep stairs up to the porch.

I knocked on the door. Sue Langtree opened it, and said, "There you are. Come on in." With that, she gave me a gigantic smile that made me want to compliment her dentist.

I stepped into the front room of the house, a formal living room with antiques and expensive furniture. Barbara sat on the sofa with my grandmother next to her holding her hand. Nana Cole looked more alert and healthier than she had in months. I wondered if tragedy was her element.

Sue crossed the room and sat down on Barbara's other side. On a loveseat, which matched the sofa, sat Jan and Dorothy. In other chairs there was Dolores from church and a few others I didn't know. I didn't see Bev anywhere.

Dolores got up and whispered to me that Cheryl Ann was in the kitchen. "The young people are making snacks."

I resisted the temptation to say, "Oh goodie."

Walking across the living room, I went through a door that led to a formal dining room, then another into the kitchen. There, I found Cheryl Ann wearing a giant MSU sweatshirt, Sheila from church, two women in their mid-thirties who I guess qualified as 'young people,' and Bev.

I glared at Bev.

"You said she looked tired. She doesn't look tired."

"Second wind," she said, shrugging. "We're making sandwiches and cookies. And iced tea. Jump in."

'Jump in' turned out to be my doing chores: washing dishes, taking out the garbage, running to Benson's Country Market for a couple pounds of luncheon meat, a few loaves of sourdough and those wonderful lemon cookies they sell. People kept arriving and I began to wonder if the death of Barbara's grandson had been nationally televised.

During the course of all this, I picked up a few details. Barbara's grandson had been gunned down while he and his unit protected an oil field in northern Iraq. Or maybe it was southern Iraq. That part was sketchy. Apparently, the fighting had been intense enough that Josh—his name was Josh—that his body was left there for several days until a mission could be organized to go back and retrieve it.

I also picked up on the fact that Josh's mother was in Wisconsin and his father in Chicago. They'd apparently divorced many years ago, leaving Josh to spend summers with his grandmother. It wasn't until I'd returned from Benson's Country Store—only to find another sink full of dishes—that anyone mentioned the fact that Josh was only nineteen.

That kind of hit me. He was about five years younger than I was. How did he end up on the other side of the world protecting someone else's oil well? Why did he think that was a good idea? Why did anyone think that was a good idea?

And then I got the feeling I was missing something, something important. I wandered back out to the living room and there, on the wall over the electric organ, were a bunch of framed photographs of Josh growing up. There were about ten of them: Josh with his grandparents, Josh alone, Josh during his summer visits. One of the photos brought me to a stop. It was me at twelve with Josh, who would have been about seven. I had no memory of the photo being taken, and very few memories of Josh at seven.

I'd been sent to spend a summer with my grandparents— believe me, I've done everything I can to block that from my memory. It was probably around the time my mother got together with Frank—and since they were newlyweds they didn't want me around much. Well, even after they were newlyweds they didn't want me around much.

Not that I can blame them. I didn't like Frank much and had made it abundantly clear. Eventually, I got better at hiding it, if only so I could stay in Los Angeles. Anyway, I was miserable that summer. Homesick and angry. And then, to make matters worse, my grandmother and Barbara would drop me and Josh off at the park—a tiny patch of green grass with a basketball court—and expect us to entertain ourselves. Basically, I took that to mean I was supposed to be this kid's babysitter.

I can't begin to tell you how unappealing a seven-year-old is to a twelve-year-old. I don't remember a lot about the times I spent with him, other than I kept trying to lose him, and somehow he managed to keep up with me. Annoying, thy name is Josh. And now he was dead. That was weird. Honestly, I didn't know a lot of dead people. And even fewer dead young people.

My grandmother was giving me the hairy eyeball and nodding toward the kitchen. Apparently, I was to get back to work. Jeez, I didn't even get a minute to feel bad about the dude dying. Still, I went back into the kitchen.

The phone rang. A lot. Sue Langtree designated herself to answer it. A couple of times it was Barbara's daughter in

Wisconsin. Apparently, she was trying to get the Army to commit to a date when Josh's body would be returned to Franklin, which was outside of Milwaukee. People were saying that was where the funeral would be held.

Reverend Wilkie showed up, which didn't exactly go down well with some people. One of the thirty-somethings in the kitchen said, "It's a shame we lost Chr—Reverend Hessel. He was always so good at this kind of thing."

"He was such a comfort when my grandmother died."

I kept trying to work my way back into the living room. I wanted to get next to Nana Cole so I could whisper into her ear that we should leave. I mean, it was almost seven o'clock.

Finally, it was Barbara herself who saved me. One of my trips out there, ostensibly looking for paper plates, she stood up in the middle of the living room, and said, "Please. You've all been so kind, but I'd really like to be alone now."

It took quite a while, but we all made our goodbyes and left. For the first few minutes Nana Cole didn't say anything. I was thinking about the endless parade of casseroles that would now show up at Barbara's door. I wondered how she'd make room for them all in her refrigerator.

Then, my grandmother said, "Thank you. Thank you for not going into the military."

"That's a weird thing to say."

"I wouldn't want to lose you. Not the way Barbara has lost her Josh."

"I thought you believed in this war."

"I do. Of course, I do."

"Just not enough to send your own grandson."

"You can believe in something and not want someone you love to die for it."

I shook my head. "I don't think so. That's not believing in something."

A few minutes later, we walked into the kitchen. The

room smelled burnt and there was a thin layer of smoke in the air. The smoke alarm was blaring.

"Shit," I said.

"Don't swear."

"I left a casserole in the oven."

"And I'm the one who needs to be watched."

CHAPTER TWENTY-THREE

It rained most of that next week. Jasper came by and talked to my grandmother in tense monosyllables about the cherries. None of it made a lick of sense to me. It had been too warm too early, and now it was raining too much. To me those sounded like perfect conditions to grow most anything. Strangely, their tense faces said otherwise.

I tried to get back on track with my hunt for Reverend Hessel's killer. I thought it was Carl Burke because he was in love with Denny, and Denny was partying and playing with his stepfather. But it wasn't Carl. So maybe it was someone else Hessel partied with. For that matter, it could be Denny. Though I doubted Denny would want to kill the goose that laid the golden egg.

I spent quite a lot of time in a couple of AOL chat rooms asking leading questions about Tina. I found several guys willing to give me meth in exchange for sex, but that was backward. I really needed to find guys who were willing to exchange sex for drugs. They were notably silent.

Then I started to wonder if there really was a parishioner who wanted to see him that night. It was possible. It was also possible that Reverend Wilkie and Sue Langtree were not the only ones at the church he'd been blackmailing. If that was true, how was I going to figure it out?

The funeral for Barbara's grandson was set for the following Monday. She was flying over to Wisconsin the day before. Sue Langtree planned a little get-together the Sunday before, right after church. With the invitation, which she made to my grandmother after another really boring service, she added, "The funeral will be all about the parents, as it should be. I thought we should take a little time for Barbara."

"Why can't Bev take you?" I asked when Nana Cole said we'd be going at two.

"Because I want you to take me."

"Fine, I'll drop you off and come back and get you."

"Do you have something else to do?"

In all honesty, I did not have anything to do. I just didn't want to spend the afternoon with a bunch of old ladies, one of whom would be doing her best not to start crying. Apparently, I had no choice.

Sue Langtree lived on Murdock, which was a block from St. Pete's where Barbara lived and two blocks from Main Street in downtown Masons Bay. The house was one of the oldest on the street and on the outside looked kind of like the house on *Charmed*. Inside, though, it was anything but charming. What it was, was fussy. Every piece of furniture had fringe or ruffles, doilies, runners, draped blankets and artfully puffed pillows. The windows were covered with sheer curtains and thick satin drapes that matched the busy wallpaper. When we walked into Sue's living room, I nearly took a step back from the shock. My grandmother took it in stride, not noticing anything, intent on using her cane.

There were little collections everywhere; figurines, matching vases, a grouping of antique dolls on a shelf, paperweights on a table in front of the picture window, and silver-plated spoons in a case. The room was full of people I didn't know. The only people I did know, or at least sort of knew, had squeezed themselves onto the over-pillowed sofa: Bekah Springer, a woman who looked enough like Bekah to be her mother—so I figured she was—and Reverend Wilkie.

Sue fluttered into the room after we let ourselves in.

"Emma, thank you for coming."

"I made my broccoli surprise," my Nana Cole said, nodding her head at me. I was holding the warm casserole in both hands. On the way, she'd explained that it was a combination of frozen broccoli, mushroom soup and Velveeta. My stomach turned at the mention of broccoli.

"Wonderful," Sue said. "Barbara is in the kitchen with the girls."

I followed them into the kitchen, only to find that it was even more crowded than the living room. Nana Cole made a beeline for Barbara and her friends sitting at the dining table, while I hugged the wall.

Barbara looked up at my grandmother, saying, "It was supposed to be over in a few weeks. They were supposed to run into the streets to welcome us. Josh was afraid he would get there and it would be over."

"We really shouldn't talk politics," Jan said. "It's never turns out well."

"Josh was a good boy," Nana Cole said. "He was a soldier, and he did his duty."

Thankfully, if I'd tried to do my duty, I'd have been booted out for being gay. I don't know why some guys think getting shot and killed in some dinky foreign country is a civil right we should worry about. I mean, there has to be some benefit to being gay, right?

I started feeling anxious. I can be a little uncomfortable in crowds. I know that might seem odd for me to say, since I've spent more than my fair share of time on Santa Monica Boulevard flitting between this bar and that, but it's true. I get nervous in crowds.

The only reason I don't get nervous at Rage or Revolver is

that I understand the currency. I'm a young, reasonably attractive guy. I'm what everyone there wants. All I need to do is spend the evening politely saying, "No, thank you, I'll pass." Or, occasionally, "Absolutely." But here, in an old lady's kitchen, I didn't know what the currency was. I didn't really know what people wanted from me. Even if I did know, I wouldn't know how to be that.

Suddenly, Bekah Springer was standing next to me. "I saw you come in."

"Hi, how are you?" I asked.

"I'm okay, I guess. It's been a weird year."

I wanted to say, 'Yeah, rape and murder will do that to you,' but I said, "Yeah," instead. Then I asked her, "Do you know where your grandmother was when Reverend Hessel was killed?"

"Oh gosh, that was a while ago."

"I know but try to think. It was a Thursday."

"Thursday? Oh, well, I think she was with me. We watch *Dawson's Creek* together."

"You and your grandmother watch *Dawson's Creek* together?" I asked doubtfully.

"My grandmother's cool. Cooler than my mother. My mother's a librarian. All she ever does is read. That's why my dad divorced her. He likes to say he's not sure she actually even noticed the divorce."

"Oh, wow."

"She did notice, though. That's when she started reading Russian novels. You know, the ones where someone kills themselves at the end."

Wanting to get away from her, I said, "I should mingle. Make sure to have the broccoli surprise. My grandmother made it."

"Oh, that sounds good."

I made my way into the living room, figuring I could kill a half an hour staring at one of the collections: figurines or paperweights. Except the living room turned out to be a mistake. Reverend Wilkie saw me and came right over, like he actually *wanted* to talk to me.

"There's a rumor going around that you're asking a lot of questions about Chris Hessel's murder."

"My grandmother asked me to," I said in my defense.

"Well, you really ought to stop. No matter who asked you to."

That kind of pissed me off, so I said, "I guess it's working out pretty well for you. I mean, that Reverend Hessel was killed and you got your job back."

"I suppose you could say that. You could also say it was God's will."

"It was God's will that a minister be murdered? That doesn't sound right."

"Chris Hessel wasn't your typical minister. You and I both know that."

I wondered what he meant by that. What exactly did he think we both knew?

"Do you remember where you were when Hessel was killed?" I asked, a tad too boldly.

"Of course, I remember. I've already been asked about it by Detective Lehmann. I was visiting my wife. Sadly, I've had to place her in a home."

I flushed. "Oh, I'm sorry. I guess."

"You don't mean that. You couldn't care less."

At that moment, his sermon about lying came to mind. Had he been serious? Is this what it's like to talk to someone being honest?

"You're right. I don't know your wife and I don't really know you. I kind of don't care."

He smiled at me as though I'd just said something extraordinarily kind.

"You may be from one of the founding families, but you didn't grow up here. You don't know these people like I do.

You won't be thanked for exposing the truth. People up here would rather live with a lie they like than a truth they don't."

And then he walked into the kitchen.

Weird. Totally weird.

Bev showed up. I did my best to stay away from her. I'd finished making calls for her and had gotten more than enough volunteers for her event. I hadn't wanted to tell her though. It was still a couple of weeks off. If she knew I was done she'd just give me something else to do. Frankly, I had enough on my plate.

I started looking for the bathroom so I could take at least one of my emergency Oxys. I opened a door off the living room and found a bedroom. I almost turned around and gave up, but then I thought, maybe? I went to the far side of the bedroom and found that there was a large bathroom shared by this bedroom and another. I went in and locked the doors on both sides.

On a set of shelves above the toilet, there was a terrifying collection of ceramic fish (most of them seeming to be leaping out of the water, so I'd guess they were suicidal fish). I unwrapped my pills and took both. I ran the water in the sink and scooped up a handful to swallow the pills. Then, I flushed the toilet, so it sounded I'd done what people usually do in a bathroom. After all, anyone could have been outside the door.

I went back out to the hallway, and then through to the kitchen. Bev had brought wine. I wasn't going to *not* have a glass, so I went over and talked to her.

"Can I have a glass?"

"Sure. How's it going with those calls?"

"I'm about halfway through," I lied.

"That's encouraging. Let me know when you're finished. I've got some other things you could be working on."

"Oh, I will. I will."

I took a big gulp of my wine—red, lots of tannins—and noticed a plate of pigs in a blanket sitting on the counter. I headed over and had two in rapid succession. They were delicious. I found myself near the dining table again, which was the last place I wanted to be. That's where Barbara and my grandmother and their friends were sitting.

"I suppose you all heard. The Supreme Court made perversion legal," Jan said. I think I'd seen something about a Texas case on my Yahoo page. Two guys having sex in their living room, which somehow got them arrested.

Jan continued, "I really can't believe it. I thought this was a Christian country."

"Jan, you don't really want this to be a Christian country," Bev said.

"Of course, I do," Jan said. "Don't be ridiculous."

"Which kind of Christian?" Bev asked.

"All of them, I guess."

"If we had a state religion, we'd have civil war within a year."

"No, we wouldn't."

"Some Christians handle snakes, some talk in tongues. Do you want the government telling you that you *have* to do those things?"

"I do not," Jan said, offended at the idea.

"Well, what if that's the state religion?"

"That would *never* happen."

"Okay, well, what if the state religion is Catholic?"

"But it wouldn't be."

"So, you'd get rid of the Catholics?"

"Of course not. My brother-in-law is Catholic."

"Then you'd just get rid of the Jews?"

"Bev! What a thing to say."

"Or the Muslims?"

That brought conversation to a halt. Jan was red-faced, obviously angry. Softly, she said, "I don't understand this conversation. It doesn't have anything to do with making perversion legal."

That's when I realized Nana Cole was staring a hole in me. Suddenly, a wave of nausea seeming to begin in my toes rose through my body. This happened sometimes with Oxy; any kind of morphine-ish pill, actually. No big deal. I just had to breathe in and out calmly. In and out. In and, oh God—

As I ran to the bathroom, I barely heard Sue Langtree saying, "We really should talk about something more pleasant. Bekah introduced me to this rock band, Newsboys. It's Christian Rock from Australia—"

And then I was shutting the bathroom door, flipping the seat to the toilet and hurling into the bowl. I retched a few times and broke into a cold sweat. In the toilet bowl was a glass of red wine, a couple of chewed up pigs in a blanket and some of what might have been the waffles I'd had for breakfast. It might have been the wine that did it. Or the pigs.

Then I noticed, floating in the middle of the mess were the two Oxys I'd just taken ten minutes before. They looked fuzzy, partly dissolved.

I thought about plucking them out of my puke—but the thought of getting bile and chewed up food all over my fingers was disgusting. There was a water glass on the sink. I could use it to sort of scoop the pills up, then quickly swallow them—uck! I'd be swallowing toilet water along with bile and regurgitated food and Oxys. Well... the toilet was obviously clean. Sue had been expecting guests. Or at least it was clean until I barfed in it. I went back to the idea of plucking the pills out with my fingers and then maybe rinsing them under the faucet...

And then I had a horrible thought. Picking a couple of Oxys out of a puke-filled toilet and swallowing them again was something an addict would do. Since I was not, definitely not, an addict, I flushed the toilet.

With great regret.

CHAPTER TWENTY-FOUR

I was on my way to find my grandmother and demand we leave, when Sue Langtree cornered me.

"You missed rehearsal this week. I was really hoping you'd come."

"I don't think singing is my thing."

"I told you before that doesn't really matter. I want you to come on Tuesday. Will you promise?"

"Uh. No."

"Oh, don't be like that. You're still new here. You need to get out and meet more people."

"I don't think 'Hi, I'm tone deaf' is great introduction."

"Oh, you silly! You're not tone deaf. Or at least you wouldn't be if you came to rehearsal. All you need is practice. Maybe a lot of it, but if you'd only try. Tuesday. Seven o'clock." After that she walked away, and I was left to go find Nana Cole. I mouthed that I wanted to leave, and she reluctantly began her goodbyes.

We left nearly an hour later. As soon as we got into the Escalade, she said, "Call Little Italy and order some fried chicken and a pizza. We'll pick it up on the way home."

Surprisingly, I was a bit hungry. I asked, "Why do they have fried chicken at a pizza place?"

"Why wouldn't they?"

"It's not Italian fried chicken, is it?"

"I don't think so. I think it's just fried chicken."

I dialed 411 and asked for Little Italy. For an extra charge, I was put through. As the phone rang, I asked my grandmother, "What kind of pizza do you want?"

"Oh, I don't care. I'm just ordering it to be polite. It would be rude to just get the chicken."

Even though that made no sense, I went ahead and ordered a bucket of the fried chicken and a meat lover's pizza, medium. For the hell of it, I added a couple of Cokes. I was told it would be about half an hour. After I hung up, we drove the five minutes to Little Italy.

Once inside, I quickly discerned that little was the more important word. Italy seemed an afterthought. There were three tables, a long counter and a giant white board as a menu —much of which was far from Italian. We were the only customers.

On the counter was a bell, which Nana Cole hit.

"She said a half an hour. It's not ready yet."

"It's only polite to tell her we're here."

After a moment, a woman in her late fifties came out. She had a wide face and thinning bangs that were meant to disguise a spider's web of scars running across most of her forehead.

"Hello Dinah, it's Emma Cole."

"Yes, Emma, I can see you."

That brought my grandmother up short. She stumbled for a moment and then meekly said, "Oh my God, I'm so sorry. I can never... this is my grandson, Henry."

I had no idea what that was about. Dinah nodded at me.

"Your order will be ready in about twenty minutes. If you let me go back into the kitchen."

"Oh. Yes, of course," my grandmother said to Dinah's back.

"What just happened?"

"Oh, I just... she has this thing. I can never remember it. It happened when she was in that awful car accident. Oh God, thirty years ago. She went through the windshield. Amazing that she—"

"What thing does she have?"

"She can't hear voices—er, I mean, she's not deaf. She can hear them, she just can't recognize them. I always think it's that she can't remember faces but it's not that, obviously. It's a brain thing."

"From the accident."

"Yes. I said that."

She hadn't exactly. Had she?

"So, everyone knows she can't recognize voices."

"Yes, but it's not polite to talk about it."

"Is this the only place you can order pizza?"

"It's good pizza. And the fried chicken—"

"Is it the only place?"

"Well, the only place in Masons Bay. There's pizza in Bell-flower. And Traverse, though I can't imagine why you'd drive forty minutes there and forty minutes—"

"Do you think this is where Reverend Hessel ordered pizza the night he died?"

"I imagine it is. I mean, it makes sense."

I stepped forward and rang the bell. After a moment, Dinah came out. She looked around and then at us.

"It's not ready yet."

"Oh, I know. I just have one question. Did you take Reverend Hessel's order the night he was killed?"

"I certainly did. I ended up stuck with a vegetarian delight."

"But you can't be certain it was him, can you?" I asked.

She glared at me. I guess I had two questions.

"He always ordered the vegetarian delight. And it was his credit card. Detective Lehmann said so."

"Don't pay any attention to him," Nana Cole said. "We'll just take our pizza and go."

"It's not ready yet," she said, clearly getting annoyed.

"So, you can tell the difference between a man and a woman?" I asked.

"Of course, I can."

She was obviously offended. I mean, I thought it was an important question.

"Why do you get to ask me something like that? I have a disability. Are you making fun of me?"

"No. I'm sorry. It's important that you actually spoke to Reverend Hessel."

"Well, I did. I'm sure I did. He coughed a lot and apologized. Apparently, he had a cold when he... died."

Did he have a cold? No one else had mentioned that.

After giving me a nasty look, she went back into the kitchen. I relaxed a little. She was really pissed off. I worried about what she might do to my pizza.

"What do you think you're doing?" Nana Cole asked.

"Well... don't you see? It might not have been Reverend Hessel who ordered the pizza."

"Why would someone pretend to be Reverend Hessel just to get a pizza? I mean, they didn't even come pick it up."

"Detective Lehmann thinks the murder happened in the time between the order being placed and when Reverend Hessel should have left to come get it. But if someone else made the call, he might have been dead already."

"But, no—"

"All they needed was his credit card information and what kind of pizza he liked. The credit card would be easy—if you killed him just take it out of his pocket."

"But knowing what kind of pizza he liked—that means it's someone who knew him," she said, her voice darkening. I could tell she hadn't quite given up on it's being a robbery or a hate crime. "You think it was Carl, don't you?"

"He'd have known what kind of pizza his stepfather liked and about Dinah's condition."

"Wouldn't that detective have checked his phone records?" she asked.

"Yes, but he could have used Opal's phone. Maybe she went to the bathroom or something."

"But why would Carl kill his stepfather?"

That was a little dicey. I didn't want to tell her that Hessel had been PNPing with a guy Carl was in love with.

"Maybe he did it for his mother," I suggested.

"Do you think they did it together?"

"I guess. I don't know. She might have found out her husband was doing drugs."

"I know women who've put up with worse," she said.

Then Dinah was back with our order: a large, flat cardboard box and a big bag on top of it. To Nana Cole she said, "You know where the napkins and forks are."

"Thank you, Dinah. And I'm sorry if Henry was rude."

"I'm just asking the questions you want answers to," I protested.

To Dinah, Nana Cole said, "Young people. They just don't get it."

MONDAY MORNING, I went to see Detective Lehmann. On the drive to the Municipal Center, I went over everything in my head again and again. I doubted Detective Lehmann would believe me. Not because what I had to say didn't make sense, but because his default position where I was concerned was disbelief.

He was there in his office. I was beginning to suspect that he left it as little as possible.

"I broke their alibi. Ivy Greene and her son."

"You 'broke' it? How did you do that?"

"My grandmother and I got a pizza from Little Italy."

"Ah, well, that makes perfect sense," he said with obvious sarcasm.

"Look, you're not from here, so you probably didn't know this. Dinah at Little Italy, she was in a car accident, went through the windshield. She has this kind of brain damage where she doesn't recognize voices. She thought it was Reverend Hessel on the phone, but it wasn't."

It was starting to make sense to him, I could tell because he looked very unhappy. "You're not from here, either. So how do you know?"

"My grandmother explained it to me."

"It was Reverend Hessel's credit card. And his credit card was still in his wallet when we found him."

"Dinah can tell men from women, but that's it. Did you get his phone records?"

"The phone records for the church should get here soon. It can take up to forty-five days. We just got the records for Ivy Greene, and they match up with what she told us."

They got phone records all the time on *Law & Order*. They usually arrived before anyone thought to ask for them. Apparently, things worked differently in real life.

"Which was?" I asked. "What did Ivy Greene tell you?"

He stared at me for a moment. "I thought you were finished with this. Didn't you tell me that?"

"Yeah, then someone tried to poison us, me, whatever."

I waited for him to decide that earned me more information. "Ivy says that Hessel called her around seven-thirty to ask if she needed him to bring anything home. She asked for the pizza."

"Or... that call came from Carl. He'd just killed his stepfather and wanted his mother's help."

"Why would Carl kill his stepfather?"

I blushed. This was going to be embarrassing. "Carl's bisexual. He's got a thing for a guy named Denny. Denny would sometimes PNP with Reverend Hessel."

"PNP? What is—"

"Seriously?" I mean, a cop would know what that meant, right? He smirked at me, happy to have gotten me riled up.

"Do you have any evidence of that?" he asked.

I decided not to mention my little trip to the local drug dealer, and went with, "I saw Denny and Carl having an argument across the street from the barbershop."

"Nothing says love like fighting on the street." He seemed to be enjoying this. "You're still just guessing."

"You could talk to Denny."

"Because drug addicts always tell the truth?"

"So, what *are* you doing next?"

"Not telling you."

CHAPTER TWENTY-FIVE

And then nothing happened. Well, not nothing exactly. The fourth of July happened. Big whoop. The Cherry Festival happened over in Traverse City. Another big whoop. I mean, we didn't go. Nana Cole was doing well with her cane but was nowhere near ready for crowds. And I had very little interest.

She did talk a lot about the festival, telling me all about the first one she went to when she was a child sometime in the Jurassic age. Then she dropped a bombshell.

"My favorite year was 1977. That was the year your mother was Cherry Queen."

"My mother was Cherry Queen?"

"Yes. I was so proud of her. She was so pretty. I really thought she was going places in life."

"She's on a yacht as we speak."

"It's not her yacht though, is it?"

That was true.

It rained most of the weekend after the fourth, so by Monday I guess it was a real disaster. My grandmother woke me up before seven. "Get up. You have to come help."

"Whaaa?"

"It's starting to rain. We could lose most of our cherries."

"What do you mean, lose? Are they going to run away?"

"They'll take up too much water and split. We have to pick them now."

"Does it really matter?"

"There won't be any money if we don't do it."

That got my attention. "What do you mean there won't be any money? I thought you were rich?"

"I'm rich because of the cherries. We can't let them get ruined."

Well, that was eye-opening.

"I'm going out there. You come as soon as you can."

A half an hour later, when I walked outside it was still barely raining. It would pick up soon, though. Soon. You could smell it in the air. The sky hung low and gray, with clouds that looked bloated and heavy. The wind was strong and turned them into a swirl. I hurried out to the orchard.

Nana Cole was already there with Jasper and a small crew of migrants. Bev and Jan were there as well. They all wore rough, cotton aprons that went over their heads and created a deep pouch over their bellies. Everyone reached up into the trees and pulled cherries down into their pouches.

Seeing me, my grandmother lurched over and handed me an apron. Honestly, even as I was getting ready and walking out, I hadn't fully connected with the idea that I would have to actually *pick* cherries. Oversee, observe, make suggestions those were all things I was prepared to do, things I was good at, but actually picking fruit? That just seemed wrong.

And then, as I snatched the first handfuls of cherries out of a tree it began to really come down. A half an hour later I was drenched, and my hands looked like Lady Macbeth's. I'd squeezed a little too hard and burst a cherry or two or twenty.

Of course I had to eat some—I hadn't had any breakfast— and the first thing you notice about eating cherries, in addition to the blood red juice all over your hands, is that they don't actually taste like cherries. Or rather, they don't taste like anything 'cherry-flavored' you've ever had. This was definitely a new experience.

Nana Cole was flitting about on her four-pronged cane. One moment she'd be picking cherries herself, next she'd be handing out aprons, offering encouragement, thanking people for coming.

Jasper would go around and take a full apron away from a worker and give them another. Then he'd take the cherries over to a large wooden box and dump them in. I kept picking. The stems kept poking my palm.

It seemed like a lot of fuss over a bunch of cherries. Yeah, I guess it meant more than that to Nana Cole. It wasn't just about the cherries, or the money. It was like her life. It was the life of her parents. And their parents. And...

And then I felt something—not the pricks in my palm, and not a big something. But something. A connection? This is what my family had done for generations. Farmed this land, pulled a living out of this soil, for a very long time. And it was something I was a part of. I'd never thought about it that way before. Now, I wasn't kidding myself. If I were able to meet my relatives, I don't know that I'd even have liked them; nor they me. But that didn't change the fact that we were part of each other. That had to mean something—didn't it?

My bag was very nearly full when I heard my grand-mother saying my name, "Henry. Henry."

"What?"

God, she was annoying.

She nodded her head and looked behind me. I turned around and there was Opal getting drenched. It was a total romantic comedy moment. You know, where someone is so in love they don't notice the weather. But one look at Opal's face told me that was not what was happening. She was anything but in love.

"What are you doing here?"

"Ivy and Carl have been arrested."

"Finally," I couldn't help saying.

"I knew it! I knew you had something to do with it." She stepped forward and slapped me on the chest. Cherries bounced out of my apron.

"Hey. Don't do that."

"You idiot. Carl didn't do it," she said stridently. "He couldn't have. He was with me."

"His alibi was faked. Hessel could have died hours earlier."

"I don't believe Carl could kill his stepfather then just come over to hang out with me. That would be heartless. He's not heartless."

"I don't know what you want me to do. Detective Lehmann would have figured it out eventually."

"No, he wouldn't have. This is all your fault."

"Did you know? Did you think—wait, you sent me to get my haircut, you wanted me to think Denny did it."

"I think Denny *did* do it."

"Why would Denny do it?"

Nana Cole came over holding a picking apron in one hand. "Hello Opal. Thank you—"

"She's not here to pick cherries," I said. "Ivy and Carl were arrested."

"Finally!" she said, surprising both Opal and me.

For a moment, I thought Opal might pound my grandmother's chest like she had mine, but she didn't. Instead, she turned and stormed off.

"Hey, don't just leave."

Without turning around, she lifted one hand and gave me the finger. It stung. Not being flipped off, but what it probably meant. Losing her friendship, I guess. She was the closest thing to a friend I had in Michigan. Or maybe anywhere.

I mean, Vinnie wasn't really talking to me. Sometimes I got calls from guys who wanted to go bar-hopping or come over and have sex. But once they found out I was in Michigan, well,

I didn't hear from them again. As though whatever purpose I'd served in their lives had ended.

But Opal... Well, yes, she was snarky and obnoxious and had an annoying habit of disagreeing with me, and all that. On the other hand, she showed up. She was there.

And now she wasn't. I was pretty sure she'd never talk to me again. Unexpectedly, that mattered.

"Henry," Nana Cole called out. "Get back to work."

About an hour later, a friend of Jasper's came by with a one-man shaker. You have seriously never seen anything like this. It's kind of like a forklift, except instead of a lift it has an upside-down canvas umbrella attached to the front. You drive it up to a cherry tree, it wraps the canvas umbrella around the tree, and then shakes all the cherries off. Everything was going to be fine. We'd done it. We'd saved the farm—or whatever.

"SO, can I have the money you promised me?" I asked Nana Cole that evening.

"Well, no."

"What do you mean no? You wanted me to ask a few questions, which I did, a long time ago. And now people have been arrested for your preacher's murder. I think you owe me."

"Who killed him? Was it Ivy or Carl?"

"They've both been arrested, so I'd guess they're in it together."

"Really? Your friend Amber seemed to think Carl is innocent."

"Her name is Opal. And just because she thinks that doesn't mean it's true. I think you need to pay me."

"And just because you think that doesn't mean I'm going to."

And then, to really spite me, she announced her intention to sit down and watch *Seventh Heaven*. That was a hard no for me, so I went upstairs. Before I did though, I snagged the most recent copy of the *Eagle* so I could look for a car and get the heck out of there. Of course, that was hopeless. I now had just a little more than five thousand—if Nana ever gave me the money she owed me. That wouldn't buy me much.

My phone rang. I flipped it open. It was Edward.

"Hey," I said in what I hoped was a sultry voice.

"Hey. I just got back from my trip. I mean, I got back a couple days ago, but I had to work. Did you have a nice holiday?"

I wanted to say I'd solved a murder but couldn't figure out if that was sexy or not. Not to mention I didn't actually know who did it, yet. All I knew was who'd been arrested, which didn't sound like me solving anything.

"Yeah, I did have a nice holiday. We watched the fireworks."

This was not a big deal since we could see them from the front porch.

"I thought about you a lot while I was gone."

"I thought about you, too." I mean, it's what I was supposed to say, right? And I did think about him. In between thinking about a whole lot of other things.

"I know it's late notice, but if you wanted to come over for a glass of wine."

Oh my God! This was a booty call. Perfect! My plan was to buy a car and drive away, so if all he wanted was to have sex, well, great! I didn't have to feel guilty that he might want to get all romantic and live happily ever after and all that.

I ran into the bathroom to take a shower, thinking, *On the other hand, maybe we will live happily ever after.* Which led to ten minutes of *Oh my God, oh my God. I'm going to marry a doctor.*

Not that we could legally get married. Well, in Hawaii, I think. And Vermont, sort of. I mean, a civil union was the same thing, right? Of course, they just legalized gay marriage in Canada a few weeks ago. Canada was closest. We'd probably go there.

We could honeymoon in Toronto, maybe? I've never been there, but they had to have gay bars, didn't they? Though, I suppose if you're married you don't *need* gay bars. But they're nice to have around. You can meet other couples or just focus on having drinks.

I had the strange, secret feeling this might work out. All I had to do was convince him to move to Los Angeles with me. Being a doctor's wife would be a huge upgrade from barista. I wondered how long it would take before he'd pay off my debts? And maybe buy me a really nice car?

Done with my shower, I dug through the closet looking for a particular T-shirt. It was just a simple black one, but it was XS which meant it clung to me like spray paint while showing off a good inch of skin at the waistband. I wore the shirt with my everyday jeans, so it didn't look too calculated.

Dr. Edward Stewart lived in a condominium sitting on a hill above Masons Bay. He was literally five minutes away, which was going to be super convenient for future booty calls. Exciting, right?

The complex was a dozen or so individual two-story buildings, each with two or three units. They had to be enormous inside. The grounds were immaculate. Obviously, when I convinced him to move to L.A. with me, we were going to have to live in Brentwood or Beverly Hills. He had taste. I drove around until I found his condo and parked behind his two-car garage.

Nervously, I walked up his sidewalk to the front door and rang the bell. A few moments later he answered the door—in nothing but a pair of jeans. His chest was wide and well-muscled with a layer of neatly trimmed dark hair.

I nearly passed out just so he could give me CPR.

Without a word he pulled me into his arms and kissed me. Oh. My. God. This was so much better than the Tina-influenced kiss I'd gotten from Denny. And I had the distinct feeling it was going to get better from here, not worse. We kissed for about as long as I could stand it and then I pushed him away to ask, "I thought we were taking this slow. What changed your mind?"

"I lost a patient. Overdose. Reminded me how fragile life is and that we need to, you know, seize the day."

Honestly, I was hoping for something along the lines of 'You're just too sexy to resist.' We're all going to die, so let's hurry up and live was not what I'd call sexy.

Edward, however, still was. Incredibly sexy. I dove back in for another long, passionate kiss. I had my hands all over his chest. He was so hot. I mean literally. I wondered if he had a fever.

He pulled me into his condo. We got exactly two feet before he was pushing me up against the wall. He slid his hands into my jeans in the back, slipping them into my underwear.

I reached down and unzipped the jeans and then tried to shimmy out of them, all the while maintaining the kiss. My jeans were mid-thigh when everything fell out of my pockets. Loose change, dollar bills, a receipt from Drip, my emergency Oxys wrapped in foil, three sticks of juicy fruit, a peppermint breath mint, my keys, stinky dog treats for Riley.

Edward looked down and laughed. He crouched down and started picking up my things.

"That's okay. Just leave it," I said. "I'll come back later."

It did kind of break the mood. He handed me my loose change. I stepped out of my jeans and put the change back in the front pocket. I wasn't sure what to do with the pants, should I fold them? Should I toss them on the floor? Or just set them so the change didn't—

I glanced at Edward and saw that he'd opened the foil on my Oxys. He looked up at me, hurt in his eyes, and asked, "Why do you have these?"

"I have a prescription," I said, reflexively.

"From Dr. Blinski?"

"Yeah. How did you know that?"

"Everybody knows what he's doing. Henry, these are dangerous. Very dangerous. They're addictive. The pharmaceutical company tells doctors they're not addictive, which is why they're so easy to get, but it's not true. It's an outright lie."

"Well, I'm not an addict," I said. "I just like having fun sometimes."

"And you carry pills around in case you have a 'fun' emergency?"

Well, that was snarky.

"What's the big deal? You gave me some."

"I gave you ten. At the lowest possible dosage. There's no reason for you to still be taking pain pills. Your ankle is fine."

"It hurts."

"The overdose I mentioned. That was Oxycontin. I watched someone die from these just a few hours ago. Henry, I can't have anything to do with this."

He gave me a look that made it clear he thought I was lying. About my ankle, about having fun, about being an addict. I hate that. I mean, yeah, I *was* lying about my ankle. But that was all. Really.

And honestly, isn't it impolite of people to notice when you're telling a tiny fib?

"If you need help, Henry, I can help you get it."

Okay, that was just gross.

I said, "You know, I'm not sure this is working out."

Unfortunately, he agreed with me.

CHAPTER TWENTY-SIX

Two days later, I had the flu. Stuffed up nose, chills, body aches, fatigue. You know the drill. I told my grandmother I wasn't feeling well, went back upstairs, and took an Oxy. Okay, two. I mean, I hadn't had one for *days*. Edward treating me like I was a raging addict took the fun out of things. But now that I was sick, it made no sense to abstain since I knew I could just sleep my symptoms away.

Anyway, that's why it took me three days to set up a visit with Ivy Greene behind bars. That, and the fact that the Wyandot County Jail had this weird, unnavigable phone system that I tried to use to schedule a half-hour visit. It took two hours to get an appointment for that Thursday at eleven in the morning.

I told my grandmother I was going to Meijer over in Traverse but drove to the Wyandot Municipal Center instead. I wasn't entirely sure where the jail was exactly, but I believed it was attached to the sheriff's office in some way.

It made sense to stop off and see Detective Lehmann for a minute. He could direct me to the jail afterward. I wasn't especially surprised when he looked up from his desk, and asked, "What are you doing here?"

"I scheduled an appointment with Ivy Greene in about fifteen minutes."

"Well, that's interesting. We let her out this morning."

"You what?"

"We can only hold someone for seventy-two hours. The prosecutor declined to charge her."

"But she didn't have an alibi. And she has a motive. What about Carl?"

"We let him go, too."

"How could you do that?"

"They lied about their whereabouts and they have motives, but that's all we have. We don't have a murder weapon. We can't place them at the scene. I brought them in to see if either of them would talk, but they had a lawyer here within the hour. Neither of them said a word."

"Doesn't that tell you something?"

"I can't charge them with silence. Not to mention, I really don't know what to charge them with. Maybe Carl killed his stepfather and his mother is helping him cover it up. Or maybe it's the other way around. Or maybe they planned it together. So murder, aiding and abetting, conspiracy to murder those are all possible. But I don't know which goes where."

"How are you going to figure it out?"

"Without one of them turning on the other, I don't know. I need witnesses; people they might have confided in, or better yet, the murder weapon."

I wondered for a moment why he was being so forth-coming to me. He usually wasn't. Then he asked, "You're friendly with that Opal girl..."

"I'm not sure friendly is the right word."

"Has she said anything about Carl's relationship with his stepfather?"

"Only that she's convinced he's not the murderer."

"If she says anything, let me know."

"Sure," I said, though honestly I wasn't sure she'd want to

talk to me ever again. And even if she did, I doubted she'd talk to me about Carl.

I walked out of the Municipal Center feeling kind of bummed. I had questions I wanted to ask Ivy. Now I wouldn't be able to ask them. Actually, that wasn't true. I knew where she lived. I could just drive to her house. She was just as likely to answer my questions there as she would have been to answer them in jail.

Fifteen minutes later, I was pulling into Ivy's driveway. I walked down the boardwalk to the fake chalet and knocked a couple of times on the awkward basement door but got no answer. I started back to the driveway but noticed Ivy down by the water. Following a nearly invisible path, I made my way down the sloping lawn.

She wore a pair of long cutoffs and a pink T-shirt. She was smoking a cigarette. When she heard me approaching, she turned and looked at me without reacting. It was almost as if she expected me.

Turning back to look out at the bay, she said, "I don't smoke. It just seemed the right thing to do after being accused of murder." She tossed the cigarette into the messy garden.

"I have a couple of questions," I said.

"Of course, you do. Opal tells us you're the one who figured out Chris didn't order the pizza himself. That he was probably already dead."

I nodded my head. "You ordered the pizza from the pay phone at Main Street Café, didn't you?"

"On the advice of my attorney, I'm not going to answer that."

"That makes it sound like you did fake your alibi. And if you faked the alibi, for you and Carl, it makes it seem like one of you killed your husband."

"Yes, I understand that." She kept staring out at the bay. It was calm. Calmer than she was. "I wish my lawyer had let me say that yesterday. I wanted to. He doesn't think I'll be believed. Or maybe he doesn't believe me. Or maybe he's just trying to run up his bill."

She stopped and seemed to think about what she wanted to say. "Chris and I had been fighting. I'd found out what he was up to. And apparently, you have too."

I nodded.

"That night, I went over to the church. I'd finally worked up enough nerve to catch him in the act. He was there. Dead. I thought— I assumed Carl had done it. That he'd found out what was happening. I had to protect him. He was already at Opal's house. I hurried over to Main Street Café, said hello to a few people then I used the pay phone and Chris's credit card number to order a pizza."

"Dinah was sure it was a man."

"I lowered my voice and spoke through my sleeve. And I pretended to have a cold."

Something about what she was saying made me ask, "You thought Carl killed your husband, but you don't think that anymore?"

"No. I actually got an attorney before we were arrested. I brought Carl with me. He was shocked that I thought he'd killed Chris. He admitted he knew about Chris and Denny, but he said he wouldn't have done it, couldn't do it. I could see he was telling the truth. I should have just called the police when I found the body. Now it looks very much like one of us killed him."

"When you found the body, did you see anything that could have been used to kill him?"

"No. I looked. But I didn't find anything."

"How exactly did you find out Reverend Hessel had a problem with drugs?"

"A few weeks before he died, a man approached me at Main Street Café. He said he was an old friend of my husband's. That he'd grown up in Fife Lake, but met Chris while they were both in prison at Stateville over in Illinois. He told me they'd shared a cell. And he told me why. The drugs and everything."

That made sense. Reverend Hessel had said he had family in the area. But he didn't. He'd come because of his prison buddy. He probably had a place to stay in Fife Lake for a short while. Before he began his long con.

Ivy had paused to think about what she was saying and what she'd say next. "I think I've been very naïve. As soon as Chris became our pastor, he began telling me he was seeing constituents in the evening. He'd come home excited by the work, energized, unable to sleep. Of course, he wasn't seeing anyone. I mean, not anyone who went to our church, at least. He was seeing young men he found on the Internet."

She took a deep cleansing breath.

"When I found out what was really happening, I confronted him. He promised to stop, said he wouldn't do it anymore. Still, I cut off his allowance."

"You gave him money?" I asked, even though I kind of already knew the answer.

"The church doesn't pay much. I thought he might stop if he didn't have money. I hoped he would. But he didn't. He'd say he had to meet someone in the evening. He'd come home excited. Except now I knew. He wasn't excited, he was high."

"Why did you think Carl had killed his stepfather?"

"One time, when Chris said he was seeing someone, I waited about a half an hour then I drove past the church. I recognized Denny's red Thunderbird. I should have confronted him then, but I didn't—"

"You knew how Carl felt about Denny?"

"Yes, of course. He's my son. I knew it was only a matter of time until he found out."

"After you cut him off, how do you think Reverend Hessel was paying for his drugs?"

"I don't know. I really thought he'd stopped. For a while."

"Did you know about Reverend Hessel blackmailing

Reverend Wilkie and Sue Langtree in order to get their positions?"

"No. I... this is the first I've heard of it. I suppose I should have guessed."

"Do you think he could have been blackmailing someone for money?"

"I suppose. It makes sense."

"Did you try to poison me?"

She blushed before she said, "I'm afraid I did. I hope you'll forgive me."

"That's really up to my grandmother. She's the one who ended up in the hospital." I fidgeted for a moment and then said, "You should tell all this to Detective Lehmann. I think your lawyer was wrong to tell you not to."

"Oh, well, in that case..." she said, sarcastically.

Maybe it was the wrong advice, I don't know. It was free though. So, there's that.

DRIVING AWAY from Ivy Greene's I was fairly convinced that Reverend Hessel had tried to blackmail someone else for money and they'd killed him. By the time I got to Masons Bay Village, I'd decided that the best way to find out who Reverend Hessel had tried to blackmail was to talk to someone who'd been blackmailed by him before.

I turned off Main Street and cut over to Murdock. When I pulled up in front of her house, Sue Langtree was on her hands and knees in the front yard. Weeding. Seeing me, she stood up and waved.

"I know why you're here," she called out when I stepped onto the sidewalk.

"You do?"

"Of course. And the answer is yes. I'll happily give you singing lessons."

"Um, no."

She looked confused for a moment and then seemed to decide not to be. "You missed choir rehearsal again. Are you here to apologize?"

"I'm not joining your choir."

"Is there something wrong with Emma?"

"I'd like to ask you some questions about Reverend Hessel. I know he blackmailed you into stepping down as choir director."

Her smiled didn't break. She said, "I suppose you should come inside. How about I make some lemonade?"

"That sounds nice," I said, following her up the walkway and into the house. She stopped at a coat rack and took off the men's flannel shirt she'd been wearing to garden.

"It was my husband's," she explained as she brushed it gently with one hand. "I still have most of his clothes. They make me feel close to him."

As she walked through the living room toward the kitchen, she said, "I've been wondering if you'd come around. People tell me you've been asking questions about Reverend Hessel. I was beginning to feel left out. Make yourself comfortable, I'll be back in two shakes of a lamb's tail."

Without a room full of people, her décor seemed even more combative. After she left, I focused on small areas, one at a time. I looked over her figurines and then the blue-and-white vases. It was when I was looking at her collection of paperweights kept in a glass table in front of the window—one filled with a flower, another with bits of glass that looked like candies, one filled with a rocking horse—that I realized... that I knew something was wrong.

I picked one up. It was as wide as my hand, clear glass, heavy, inside it held musical notes. Had I seen it before? Was it in the photograph of Reverend Hessel sitting at his desk? Was it the same paperweight or one just like it? I thought back to the box of Hessel's things in his old office. I didn't remember seeing a paperweight in there, so maybe this was the same one.

Sue came into the living room with a tray of lemonade and cookies, setting them on the coffee table. As she did, I wracked my brain trying to remember her alibi. And then I realized something I should have known all along.

"*Dawson's Creek* is on Wednesdays."

"Yes, I know. I watch it with my granddaughter, Bekah. We just love it."

"She told me that's what you were doing the night Reverend Hessel was murdered. He was killed on a Thursday."

"I suppose we were watching something else then," she said. Then she glanced down at the musical paperweight I still held in my hand. "They're worthless, you know. People don't really use paperweights anymore. We don't use paper the way we once did. The one you're holding is my favorite."

"You gave one that looked like this to Reverend Hessel."

"I did. How remarkable that you noticed." She took it from me and caressed it like it was a pet of some sort. "We were friends, you see. When Chris first arrived. He was very helpful with the choir—at first. I gave him this one as a gift."

"He gave it back to you?"

"No. I killed him with it. There's a certain sort of irony in that, I suppose. It was sitting on his desk. I had brought the cash he wanted. Five thousand dollars. Well, not really. I had two one-hundred-dollar bills and I cut up some newspaper— anyway, that's not all that interesting. I dropped it, you see. I thought... I knew he'd pick it up. I was right. He wanted the money so much. He bent over and that's when I took the paperweight off his desk and hit him on the back of the head. I did it again. And again. Until he fell to the floor. It was much easier than I'd have thought."

"You should be confessing to Detective Lehmann."

"Oh, I'm not going to do that." She turned and picked up a

glass of lemonade to hand to me. "Would you like a cookie? I made them this morning."

"Aren't you afraid I'll tell Lehmann what you said?"

"Not really. No."

"But I will tell him."

"You won't. If you do, everyone will find out that my granddaughter was raped. And that we... did what was necessary. It will hurt innocent people. Like my Bekah. She's a sweet girl, isn't she?"

"Not telling will hurt innocent people, too. Ivy Greene and her son were in jail. People will think they did it."

"But they didn't do it. That's why they were released. There wasn't enough evidence. Reverend Wilkie and I have started a legal defense fund for them. Just in case. You don't need to worry. They'll be fine."

Lehmann knew he didn't have much on them. Since they didn't do it, I doubted he'd be able to find any more evidence.

"You're too young to know this, but the longer you live the more important it becomes to do good in this world. Sometimes good is not what you expect it to be."

"You think you did good by killing Reverend Hessel?"

"Oh yes, without a doubt."

CHAPTER TWENTY-SEVEN

A couple of days later—yes, it took me that long to make up my mind—I got up very early and drove to the Municipal Center. They weren't open yet. I sat in the Escalade until I saw a crumbling blue Subaru wagon pull into the parking lot. I climbed out of the Escalade and walked over.

Detective Lehmann rolled down his window and said, "Go away."

"I know who did it."

"So, do I. I arrested Donny Hyslip last night."

The name sounded familiar, but I couldn't place it.

"You arrested who?"

"High school senior. We found the paperweight from Hessel's desk in his room. Along with a bloody shirt."

Oh my God. He was the boy who'd raped Bekah Springer. And then I knew what had happened. Sue Langtree had put the paperweight in his room. But what about the—she'd been wearing a man's shirt when I went to see her. One of her husband's. She must have been wearing one when she killed Reverend Hessel. And she put it—

"How did you know to look for those things?"

"Girl at school turned him in. Said he bragged to her about it."

"Bekah Springer?"

"How did you know that?"

"Bekah's the only high school student I've met up here. It was a lucky guess."

He still looked at me suspiciously.

"The Hyslips are trying to say the evidence was planted. Apparently, they leave their doors open. But then, everyone up here does," he said.

"Yeah, people need to stop doing that."

———

WHAT EXACTLY IS A GOOD PERSON? And, more importantly, is it worth being one? Sue Langtree thought she was a good person. Donny Hyslip was definitely a bad person. But Sue was guilty and Donny was innocent—at least of the crime he was in jail for. I guess it was justice of a sort.

Honestly, I needed to get out of Wyandot County. It was time for me to go home, my real home. That was the only answer. I decided it didn't matter if I bought a car. In fact, I should just collect my money from my grandmother, get a plane ticket, and leave. I could get a *semi* decent used car when I got to Los Angeles.

When I got home—I mean, when I got to my grandmother's—it wasn't *my* home I reminded myself—I found her sitting in the kitchen waiting for me.

"Where have you been?"

"I went to see Detective Lehmann. They've arrested Donny Hyslip for Reverend Hessel's murder."

"Donny Hyslip? He's just a boy."

"Teenager."

"Oh. Drugs, wasn't it?"

"Um, sure... I guess."

"And now you want your money."

"Yes, I do."

"I've been talking to your mother about your hospital bill," she began. "Her friend found out that if you're poor and without insurance in California you don't have to pay more than Medicaid rates. He spoke to the hospital and got your bill reduced to fourteen hundred dollars."

Then she held out a check. I grabbed it. Even though the handwriting was that of an emotionally disturbed child, I could still clearly read that it was for five hundred forty-one dollars and thirty-eight cents. My mother had managed to not pay a dime and my grandmother—

"I paid the bill for you."

"This isn't what we agreed to. You were going to give *me* two thousand dollars. Not some hospital."

"No, but I think it's close enough." She watched me carefully for a moment. "Doesn't it feel good to be out of debt?"

"But I'm not out of debt. I still have a student loan in default and credit cards that are maxed, not to mention another hospital bill from when I got run off the road. That hasn't even arrived yet."

"Well, maybe you'll get lucky and someone else will die," she said with a bitter smile.

"You're better. You can take care of yourself. It's time for me to go back to California."

"You really think that's a good idea?"

"I do. I never wanted to be here in the first place."

"I know you're still taking those pills. I can get you help. If you want it."

Jesus Christ. That's twice in what, a week or so? Twice that someone's offered to get me help. But I wasn't—or was I? Had I accidentally gotten addicted? Was I not just having fun anymore? And how was I supposed to figure it out?

Well, obviously, I should just stop. I didn't *need* to take pills. It wouldn't be that hard. All I had to do was not take them anymore. Simple.

Then she said the oddest thing. "I'm going to leave you the farm. Your mother doesn't want it. I think, well I think you're smarter than you know. You could do very well for yourself."

As a farmer? She couldn't possibly—

"But if you go back to L.A. you won't stop with the pills. And you'll die."

"That's not true."

For a bit, she didn't say anything else. The room was very still. She stared at me, her eyes so brown, like my mothers, like mine. After taking a deep breath, she said, "While I still have the chance, I want to say thank you for the things you've done for me, taking care of me the way you have."

"I'm not very good at it."

"Well, I won't fight you on that, but you stayed and you did what was needed. That's what's important. So, thank you." She got up, leaning on her cane, then added, "I think it's time for a little nap in front of the TV." And she wobbled out of the room.

What the—I'm sure I was standing there with my mouth open. It was all too much to take in. I needed to go upstairs and take—But that's what an addict would do. Take a pill and make it all go away.

And in that moment, it was the only thing in the world I truly wanted.

Crap.

ABOUT THE AUTHOR

Marshall Thornton writes several popular mystery series, most notably the *Boystown Mysteries* and the *Pinx Video Mysteries*. He has won the Lambda Award for Gay Mystery three times. HIs books *Femme* and *Code Name Liberty* were Lambda finalists for Best Gay Romance. Other books include *My Favorite Uncle*, *The Ghost Slept Over* and *Fathers of the Bride*. He holds an MFA in Screenwriting from UCLA.

ALSO BY MARSHALL THORNTON

IN THE BOYSTOWN MYSTERIES SERIES

The Boystown Prequels

(Little Boy Dead & Little Boy Afraid)

Boystown: Three Nick Nowak Mysteries

Boystown 2: Three More Nick Nowak Mysteries

Boystown 3: Two Nick Nowak Novellas

Boystown 4: A Time for Secrets

Boystown 5: Murder Book

Boystown 6: From the Ashes

Boystown 7: Bloodlines

Boystown 8: The Lies That Bind

Boystown 9: Lucky Days

Boystown 10: Gifts Given

Boystown 11: Heart's Desire

Boystown 12: Broken Cord

Boystown 13: Fade Out

IN THE PINX VIDEO MYSTERIES SERIES

Night Drop

Hidden Treasures

Late Fees

Rewind

Cash Out

OTHER BOOKS

The Perils of Praline

Desert Run

Full Release

The Ghost Slept Over

My Favorite Uncle

Femme

Praline Goes to Washington

Aunt Belle's Time Travel & Collectibles

Masc

Never Rest

Year of the Rat

Fathers of the Bride